The United States Marshals Service

Formed in 1789 by President George Washington, the United States Marshals Service is the oldest federal law enforcement agency—and in my mind, one of the most mysterious. They used to carry out death sentences, catch counterfeiters—even take the national census. According to their Web site, "At virtually every significant point over the years where Constitutional principles or the force of law have been challenged, the marshals were there—and they prevailed." Now the agency primarily focuses on fugitive investigation, prisoner/alien transportation, prisoner management, court security and witness security.

No big mystery there, you say? When I started this series, I didn't think so, either. Intending to nail the details, I marched down to my local marshals' office for an afternoon that will stay with me forever.

After learning the agency's history and being briefed on day-to-day operations, I was taken on a tour. I saw an impressive courtroom and a prisoner holding cell—not a good place to be! Then we went to the garage to see vehicles and bulletproof vests and guns! Sure, I'm an author, but I'm primarily a mom and wife. I bake cookies and find hubby's always-lost belt. Remind my daughter's cheerleading squad which bow to wear. Nothing made the U.S. Marshals Service spring to life for me more than seeing those weapons—and I'm talking serious weapons! And then I glanced at my tour guide and realized that this guy wasn't fictional, but used those guns, put his very life on the line protecting me and my family and the rest of this city, county and state. I had chills.

Things really got interesting when I started digging for information on the Witness Security Program. Deputy Marshal Rick ever so politely sidestepped my every question. I found out nothing! Not where the base of operations is located, not which marshals are assigned to the program, where/who those marshals report to on a daily basis, what size crews are used, how their shifts are rotated—nothing! After a while it got to be a game. One it was obvious I'd lose!

Honestly, all this mystery probably makes for better fiction. I don't want to know what really happens. It's probably not half as romantic as the images of these great protectors I've conjured in my mind. Oh, and another bonus to my tour—Deputy Marshal Rick was Harlequin American Romance-hero hot!

Laura Altom

Dear Reader,

I grew up reading Harlequin romances, and after the birth of my twins, I decided to try writing them. So far—knock on wood—that seems to be working out. But even after immersing myself in all of those happy endings, only now have I truly understood the healing power of these constantly underrated books.

At the time of wrapping up this story, my husband and I have weathered what has been one of our toughest storms in over seventeen years of marriage. Coping with my husband's grandmother's advancing dementia, we've made the decision to welcome her into our home—only, our current home isn't big enough, so we're in the process of moving. With two preteens, our finances have always been tight, but now especially so. I've taken on a second job to help make ends meet.

Times have been tough. I used to be fortunate enough to spend my days leisurely writing. I now, like so many of you, hustle off to work. I squeeze in writing between cooking and laundry and chauffeuring kids to their many activities. At first I wasn't sure how I was going to fit it all in, but gradually everything began to click.

I found myself enjoying my job and my new coworkers. Most of all, I enjoyed my newly concentrated writing time. No longer able to take all day to reach my goals, I had to write faster, leaner, with an intensity I'd never before known. Through that growth, I found myself utterly caught up in Caleb and Allie's story. Might sound corny, but through their healing, I slowly healed. And instead of being afraid I won't be able to meet my next writing deadline, I now view that looming date as an exciting mountain to be conquered. Am I still scared? You bet! But knowing I have the healing power of romance to help get me through long days somehow makes it all better.

Long live Harlequin Books!

Laura Marie Altom

P.S. You can reach me through my Web site at www.lauramariealtom.com or write to me at P.O. Box 2074, Tulsa, OK 74101.

Marrying THE MARSHAL

LAURA MARIE ALTOM

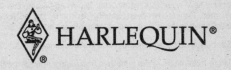

HARLEQUIN®

TORONTO • NEW YORK • LONDON
AMSTERDAM • PARIS • SYDNEY • HAMBURG
STOCKHOLM • ATHENS • TOKYO • MILAN • MADRID
PRAGUE • WARSAW • BUDAPEST • AUCKLAND

ISBN 0-373-75103-6

MARRYING THE MARSHAL

www.eHarlequin.com

Printed in U.S.A.

For United States Marshal Timothy D. Welch and
Deputy U.S. Marshal Rick Holden. Thank you for the
incredible tour of Tulsa's marshal's office, and for
patiently answering my gazillion questions!
Any technical errors are all mine!

And for my new friend and the sharpest dressed T.A.
at Nimitz Middle School, Ms. Jana King! Thank you for
making me feel at home since the first day we met,
and for always being generous with your smiles.
You are a treasure I hope to forever keep!

Books by Laura Marie Altom

HARLEQUIN AMERICAN ROMANCE

940—BLIND LUCK BRIDE
976—INHERITED: ONE BABY!
1028—BABIES AND BADGES
1043—SANTA BABY
1074—TEMPORARY DAD
1086—SAVING JOE*

*U.S. Marshals

Prologue

Nine years ago...

Caleb Logue hadn't felt this good since...

Well, since maybe never.

With his girl—soon to be wife—Allie carrying his son or daughter, he felt like he'd won the lottery. Hit the jackpot. His ship had finally come in. Tonight was going to be magic. The ring was in his front pocket. A single, flawless red rose occupied the seat beside him.

In a perfect world, she'd be getting a huge bouquet. A diamond solitaire the size of a Hershey's Kiss. As it was, her rock was more like a dust speck, but surely this was one case where it wasn't the size of the stone that counted, but the depth of his love.

That might sound corny, but what the hell? It wasn't like anyone was around to read his mind.

He loved her.

Loved her so much it sometimes hurt to think what his life might be like without her.

Lucky for him that after tonight, once she said yes

to his proposal, they'd be together for a good, long while.

In the driveway of her rented house, he turned off his crotchety Chevy pickup, then popped open the equally cranky door.

Granted, when Allie first told him she was pregnant, he hadn't taken the news all that well. He didn't think she fully understood just how much the news had freaked him out, but tonight, he'd make up for his less than enthusiastic first response. Both juniors at the University of Oregon's law school, they weren't exactly in the best financial shape to start a family.

He snatched the rose, patted his pocket to make sure her ring was still safe inside, then whistled all the way to Allie's front door.

He waved at the frat guys next door who'd moved their sofa outside to enjoy the unseasonably warm April weather. Gritty Pearl Jam played on a radio they'd set in the open front window. Their barbecue smelled great. Chicken. Just that morning, at a campus yard sale, he'd picked up a hibachi for Allie. Her rusted-out grill had seen better days.

The frat guys nodded and waved back.

Caleb reached Allie's front porch. The balmy breeze flapped the screen on the window over the kitchen sink. He'd fix it for her this weekend.

He tried walking in as usual, but the door was locked. He had a key, but it was back in the truck, so he just knocked again.

When a few minutes passed with still no answer, he loped back to the truck for the key. He slipped it into the lock, hoping the worry settling in his gut was unfounded. Allie was always home from class by now. She worked as a waitress down at McGinty's, but two nights earlier, he'd doubled-checked with her boss that she was off tonight.

"Al?" he called out while pushing open the door. "You all righ—"

He froze.

One foot inside, one out.

The once cheerfully cluttered home, filled with books and newspapers and rumpled old furniture and thriving plants, was empty. The place was no longer a home, but merely a house. Sun that usually slanted through windows, giving the wood floors a honeyed glow, now highlighted dingy walls crying for fresh paint and scuffed floors that could only be helped by hiding them with wall-to-wall carpet.

"Allie?" His pulse began to race.

What was going on?

Where could she be?

He searched everywhere. The bedroom where they made love. The kitchen where they cooked together, laughed together. The bathroom where they'd showered together. All empty.

So what now? Wait? Sit around hoping she'd come back?

At first he'd been scared, confused.

Now, he was pissed.

She hadn't been robbed. Aliens hadn't sucked up all of Allie's stuff. She'd moved it. Deliberately and coldly and calculatingly moved it.

To get away from him?

Obviously. But why? She was carrying his baby. What had he ever done but loved her?

He locked up, headed for his truck.

"If you're lookin' for Al," one of the frat guys shouted, "we helped her load the last of her stuff this morning."

Hand to his forehead, shading his eyes from the setting sun, Caleb asked, "She say where she was going?"

"Nah."

Caleb muttered a quick thanks, and headed for his apartment—used more as a storage shed than shelter. Allie's place had basically been his home, but her mom was old-fashioned, Allie had said. She wouldn't have understood them living together before marriage.

Caleb mechanically got through the weekend.

Monday morning, he somehow made it to class.

Caleb's dad was a retired U.S. Marshal. Now, sheriff of their small, coastal Oregon hometown. Vince Logue had made a few inquiries on behalf of his son, but for all practical purposes, Allie had vanished. Caleb finally resorted to calling the mom who hadn't approved of him. Her words of wisdom were to leave her daughter alone.

Monday afternoon, Caleb snatched the mail from his box.

Nestled amongst bills and credit card applications was a letter.

Dear Caleb—
Sorry for taking off like I did, but I didn't know what else to do. I lost the baby, but before that, I

could already tell I'd lost you. The look in your eyes after I'd told you my news, it told me the last thing you wanted to be was a father. I don't blame you. My being pregnant was a shock to me, too.

But what also came as a shock was your apparent lack of feeling for me. I always assumed we'd end up together, but guess I was wrong. And that's okay. I mean, I'm hurt, but I understand, and willingly grant you your freedom. Maybe my losing the baby was somehow a blessing. Maybe if I hadn't, you might've felt forced into "making it right," like you said you would do. But what you have to understand is that I don't want to spend the rest of my life with a man who makes my life "right," but magical. I want the fairy tale, Caleb. I want love.

Please don't try to find me. I think it's for the best that we both go our separate ways. Good luck in your future. I wish you well in all you do. Allie

Caleb read the letter four times, then wadded it into a ball he deep-sixed into the trash.

He went out for a couple beers.

Came home.

But the apartment had never been his home. He fell onto the sofa and cried. And when he'd finished, he snatched her letter from the trash, smoothed it against his chest and then sat back down on the sofa to wonder where the hell things had gone wrong.

He laughed.

His first mistake? Hooking up with a woman whose heart was made of ice.

Chapter One

"Sorry, sir, but no can do." Portland-based Deputy U.S. Marshal Caleb Logue handed the fax with his next assignment back to his boss. Granted, Franks knew his job and was the presidentially appointed U.S. Marshal for all of Oregon, but surely even he'd understand that this—

"'Scuse me?" Franks's wooly-worm eyebrows raised and his thick neck turned red. Even at fifty, the guy still bench-pressed two-eighty.

"Sir…" Caleb gulped, but held his ground. "I know this judge. We went out for a while in college. I really think it'd be best if someone else was assigned to—"

"Ordinarily," his boss said, "I'd agree. But with Mason and Wolcheck in Texas, Villetti in Michigan, and Smith in New Orleans, I got no one else to give this to. As is, you're going to have to pull in a whole new team from other offices. Feel free to appoint someone else as our lady judge's primary sidekick, but make no mistake, you will be a key player. *Capiche?*"

Elbows on his cluttered desk, Caleb cradled his forehead in his hands.

No way this was happening.

No freakin' way.

"Glad you're on board, Logue. Get together a twelve-man team—I want six on her and four on her son at all times, two off—then haul ass down to Calumet City. This has to be in place by the end of the day. And I'm talking end of the business day—not midnight."

"Yes, sir."

ALLIE HAYWORTH looked up from her organized desk, wishing her life could be as tidy. "Watcha' doin?" she asked her eight-year-old son, Cal.

"Playin' Legos."

"I can see that," she said, rising to cross to the far side of her office where he sat on the floor. By U.S. District Court Judge standards, the space wasn't all that attractive. The burgundy leather sofa had a tear she'd duct-taped, then covered with a throw pillow. The white drapes, carpet and ceiling had a faint yellow hue and smoky smell from the judge who'd served before her—an avid cigar smoker. In a dream world where she had plenty of free time, she'd love to paint the space some vibrant, exciting color. Cobalt-blue or jungle-green. Still, floor-to-ceiling mahogany bookshelves added warmth to the overall feel, as did the fresh flowers she collected from her cutting garden at least once a week in the spring through early fall.

Her current bouquet had seen better days. The snapdragons looked tired. For this year, the growing season had ended. Would she be around for next year?

Squelching the macabre line of thought, she forced a smile, saying to her son, "Guess I should've asked what you're *making*."

"What do you think?"

"I dunno." Glad she'd worn slacks, she plunked down beside him. "A boat? Upside-down skyscraper?"

"Mo-om."

"What?" she asked, ruffling his short dark hair.

"Don't you know anything?" With dusky-green eyes that reminded her of dried sage, he gave her *the look*. The one that said despite the fact she was one of the state's youngest federal judges—not to mention, a female—that he was and would always be *wa-aa-aay* smarter than her!

"Yep," she said with a heavy sigh. "You must be right. Guess I don't know anything. So? Help me out. What are you building?"

"It's a gun." He picked up the monolithic mix of colorful blocks only to pop to his feet, then run to the window and start *shooting*. "Pow, pow!"

Allie cringed. "Caleb, get away from the windows."

"How come? The cops are right outside. No one can get us up here."

If only that were true.

Allie scrambled to her feet and drew him back, safely out of view, before closing the drapes on the low-hanging clouds and persistent rain. "I, um, appreciate you looking out for us, but why don't you leave the shooting to police."

"What're they gonna do? They've been protecting us a whole two days and still haven't caught the bad guys."

"I know, baby, but they will. Real soon."

"This is boring," Cal said, slamming his gun hard into the plastic Lego tub. His creation shattered. "I wanna go to school. Henry's bringing his dad for show and tell. He makes donuts for his job and we were gonna get free ones and everything."

"I'm sorry," she said, drawing him into a hug. "But remember how we talked about this? And decided it would be safer if you just hung out with me?"

"Yeah, but—"

A knock sounded at the door.

Allie jumped, then felt silly when her elderly secretary poked her head in. Guess being used for target practice set a girl on edge.

"Allie, hon, there's a gentleman here to see you from Portland. He's with the U.S. Marshals. Shall I send him in?"

"Of course," Allie said, releasing her son to smooth her hair and straighten her aqua silk blouse. At first she'd been opposed to having the big dogs called in, especially on the off chance her and Cal's father's paths should cross. But after this morning's latest attempt on her life, she was relieved help had arrived.

Usually, federal courthouses had marshals' offices right inside. Hers was no different, except the marshals were actually local policemen who'd been deputized into service. Not that they didn't do a fine job—after all, she was still alive. But seeing how their usually peaceful district had never had something this serious happen, they were rusty on evasive maneuvers.

Apparently the members of the white supremacist organization intent on taking her life were not.

"Baby," she said to her son. "Could you please make me an airplane while I talk to this man? A great, big one with maybe a swimming pool in first class, and—"

"Allie."

She looked to the door and her pulse went haywire. *Caleb?*

Of all the luck….

It'd been nine years since she'd last seen him. For nine years she'd told herself she hated him. Never wanted to see him again. She'd told herself every morning and night that what she'd done, what she'd kept from him, had been for good reason.

She made the mistake of meeting his direct stare. The exact shade of dried sage….

Her gig was up.

Caleb locked eyes with his son. Took a half step back, as if the air had been kicked from his lungs. But then his initial composure returned. Sort of. If you didn't count the tightening of his jaw or the way his eyes narrowed with instantaneous rage. He'd just found out the baby she'd told him she'd lost was alive and well and making an airplane out of Legos.

"This is—no." The man Allie had loved with a some-times frightening intensity gave her a hard look, then shook his head. "We're not going to do this now. Not here. In front of…" Those gorgeous, all-too-familiar eyes of his welled with tears. "How could you, Allie?" He pressed the heel of his right hand against one eye, then the other, and cleared his throat. "Your honor, my name is Caleb Logue. I'll be heading your security team."

"Oh, Caleb," she said, fighting past her own wall of tears. "I didn't mean for this to—"

"As soon as you and your boy are ready to head home, I'll accompany you."

"Please, let me…explain." Too late. He was already out the door.

"Who was that?" her son asked.

Your father.

CALEB COULDN'T BREATHE.

"Dang, Logue," his old pal from the Seattle office, Owen Richards, said. "You look like the Stay Puft Marshmallow Man—only whiter."

"Thanks." Caleb brushed past him toward the group of guys still out in the hall, who were feeling up a snack machine.

"Damned thing stole my quarter," his younger brother, Adam, complained.

"Stow it," Caleb said. "Everyone ready to rock?"

"Not without my quarter." Adam gave the machine another thump, then switched tactics by sticking his hand up the lady's metal skirt. "What bug crawled up your behind?"

What bug? Caleb snorted.

The one that came with finding out the woman he'd thought he loved was a lying, conniving wench who's still as freakin' gorgeous as ever and had bore him a damned good-looking son she didn't even have the decency to tell him existed!

"THANKS FOR THE GRUB," Adam said.

"You're welcome." Allie stood at her black granite kitchen counter, wiping grease splatters from the burgers she'd fried for dinner.

Burgers, boxed macaroni and cheese, and frozen peas.

Her mother would report her to some government agency for cooking such a lackluster meal. But then her mother had been a stay-at-home mom. She also had never received death threats. She had, however, had a policeman husband killed in the line of duty. Meaning that though she wished Allie had told Caleb about his son, she'd always been sympathetic to her daughter's rationale for keeping Cal's paternity a closely guarded secret.

Allie's dad had been shot when she was just twelve. For years, she'd bitterly wished she'd never even known him, rather than to have loved him so fiercely only to lose him in such a useless, tragic way. Wanting to protect her son from suffering the same kind of loss, she'd done Cal a favor by never letting him get attached to his adrenaline-junkie father.

Adam asked, "Got any idea what Caleb's so PO'd about?"

"None at all." Allie scrubbed harder, thankful for the fact that while she'd always liked Adam, he'd never been that big on personal observations.

"Got any ice cream?"

"Cookie dough and cotton candy."

He winced. "Guess those'll do."

She shot him a look. "You always this professional?"

"Give me a break. It's not like I don't know you. And anyway, Caleb's loaded for bear. Trust me, ain't no one gettin' through him."

"So he's out there, then?" she asked, grabbing a bowl and the ice-cream spade on her way to the freezer.

"Yup. Right outside. Along with four other marshals."

"That's nice."

"Nice?" He laughed. "Between them, they've got the firepower of a small country. Ain't nothin' nice about 'em."

"Sorry," she said, licking a sweet smudge of ice cream from her pinkie. "Didn't mean to insult your arms supply."

"S'okay."

She handed him the bowl and a spoon. "So, is um, Caleb going to be inside at all?"

"Outlook doubtful—mmm, this is better than I'd expected. Thanks."

"Sure. So, is there any time I might talk with him?"

"I guess."

Was Adam really this dense? Couldn't he see how much she needed to speak with his brother? While she didn't for a minute believe she'd done the wrong thing in shielding her son from the certain disaster that was part of Caleb's job description, she'd always felt wretched about her decision.

If only she could explain. To Caleb. To *herself.*

"Okay," she said, hands on her hips, taking a deep breath. Time for a more direct approach. "Might it be possible for you to ask Caleb to come inside right now?"

"I'm eating my ice cream."

Apparently, yes, Adam was that dense.

"MY BROTHER SAID you wanted to see me." Caleb found Allie curled in an overstuffed lounge chair, reading court documents by the light of an artsy-fartsy lamp. In a swanky marble, brass and glass fireplace, a gas flame scorched politically correct concrete logs. Call him environmentally challenged, but he'd always been partial to wood. But then wood was a good, honest material. The woman seated before him could be called lots of things. Honest wasn't one of them.

"Oh," she said, her voice as flat as her eyes. "Hi."

Not in the mood for forced pleasantries, he asked, "Our son in bed?"

She swallowed hard, then nodded. "Please, have a seat."

"I'd rather stand."

"You off duty?" she politely asked.

"Cut the chitchat, Al. You not only lied about losing my son, you didn't even have the decency to lie to my face. You took the coward's way out by doing it in a *Dear John*."

"Caleb, if you'd just let me explain."

"Explain?" He laughed. "Oh, I've spent the past nine years of my life mourning the loss of your—our—child and you're going to explain?" He thumped the red fireplace wall in anger.

"I'm sorry," Allie said. Tears were pouring down her face. "You were so focused. All you ever talked about was getting your silver star. It was an obsession. As if, along with your fascination for those awful spaghetti westerns, you were going to become part of some modern-day posse. I knew if I told you I wanted to keep the baby, you'd do the honorable thing and marry me. You'd probably even have given up your dreams. Taken some boring desk job. You'd have been miserable."

"Don't give me that. Seriously, Allie, you're a highly intelligent woman. Surely you can come up with a better excuse for a keeping a father from his son. A son from his father. You think every marshal spends every day shootin' up the hills? You think my own father ordered me and my two brothers and sister from the back of the Sears catalogue?"

"I—I said I was sorry." Allie rose, went to him, tried to give him a hug, but he backed away. Just out of reach.

"Yeah," he said, jaw hard, eyes harder. "I'll just bet."

Allie winced from the obvious disgust behind his words, winced harder at the slam of the door as he left the room.

Sure, he'd had a right to know about his son, but she had rights, too. Intrinsic rights to security and well-being and happiness and love. How convenient Caleb had managed to block out how many of her hopes and dreams he'd squashed. Did he even remember what'd *really* happened nine years ago on the night she'd told him she was pregnant?

She did. Remembered it like it was yesterday....

THE NIGHT HAD BEEN rainy, yet hot, making the air heavy.

"Damn, this is quite a spread," he'd said.

"Thanks." She'd been warmed by Caleb having noticed she'd gone to extra trouble. Wildflowers picked in the empty lot behind her rented house graced an antique Ball canning jar he'd bought for her at a flea market. He was always doing that. Finding her little odds and ends to fill her home—their home. They'd met their junior year in college. And now, their third year of law school, she'd supposed it was time for what she was about to tell him.

True, there could have been a better time for this to happen—say, after graduation when they'd both found great jobs. But you couldn't always plan a pregnancy, and there wasn't much they could do about it, other than fast forward the marriage plans they'd each hinted at.

"What's the occasion?" he'd asked, stepping up behind her at the stove, wrapping his arms around her waist, kissing the sensitive spot on the nape of her neck.

"Patience, counselor."

He'd laughed. "Right. Trial lawyer I will never be. You know why I'm going after the fancy degree."

Her heart had plummeted. So much for her wish for a lovely surprise from him. Something like a spontaneous proposal, then a heartfelt vow to not go into the marshals' service.

"You just watch." With his chest puffed out the way it always was when he talked about his career plans, he'd said, "Once I get this law degree behind me, then combine it with a stellar field service record, no mere Deputy Marshal status for me, darlin'. I'll be the youngest presidentially appointed U.S. Marshal ever in the state. You can be the youngest U.S. District Court Judge."

"Great."

"Doesn't sound good to you?" He'd swept aside her long hair, kissing a partial ring around her throat.

"Caleb, hon, I was going to wait until after dinner to tell you, but—"

Hands still around her waist, he'd turned her to face him. "Wait a minute. I know this pouty look. You bomb Valerio's midterm?"

"No," she'd said, suddenly overcome with emotion. Tears had started and wouldn't stop.

"Damn, sweetie. What's wrong?" He'd held her close, protecting her from the world. Trouble was, the thing hurting her worst was him.

"I—I'm pregnant," she'd blurted. Hoping, praying, he'd propose on the spot.

Instead, he'd gripped her tighter, like she'd fallen overboard and he was dragging her back to an already sinking ship. "This shouldn't be scary," he'd said. "But it is. I mean, I want to be a dad. A lot. But right now?" He'd shaken his head. "We've both got full plates."

"Sure." Nodding against his chest, she'd felt his frantic heartbeat.

"We'll make it right though, okay?" He'd tucked his fingers under her chin, raising it so that her gaze met his. "We'll make it right."

HE'D SAID *Make it right* all those years ago.

What had his words meant? That hadn't been the way the night was supposed to have gone. Caleb was supposed to have proposed. Tell her he loved her and their baby more than life. And he could have told her, that minute, because he loved her, he'd give up his dangerous career in favor of something nice and safe. Maybe tax law. He, better than anyone, from their many late night talks, knew what had happened to her father. And how fearful she was of tragedy striking another man she loved. Because Caleb knew, he *should* understand her actions, but didn't. In the end, the only thing he'd given up was her—*them*.

So she'd formed a plan.

One that had allowed her to keep her precious child, and Caleb to keep his apparently equally precious unfettered bachelor life and crazy-dangerous career.

Chapter Two

"Hey, it's cool that we have kinda the same name. Can I see your badge?" Caleb's son asked bright and early Monday morning.

"Sure." Caleb slipped it off his utility belt for the little boy to inspect. He was a good-looking kid. Seemed smart. Inquisitive. Interesting that he was an early riser. So was his dad.

Outside, behind the closed kitchen shades, rain drummed on the patio and deck.

"Thanks," the boy said, returning Caleb's silver star. "Want cereal? We got Cheerios and Life."

"That's okay, buddy. I'm on the job. But I appreciate the offer." After a few seconds of watching his son noisily get a bowl and spoon, he asked, "Ever eat oatmeal?"

"Yeah. I like it, but Mom doesn't make it that often."

"When I was your age," Caleb said, "my mom made it for me nearly every day—especially when it was cold. It was my favorite. Ask your mom to make it for you. She knows my recipe."

"Okay," Cal said, fetching a bright yellow cereal box from the pantry.

Was it presumptuous to think Allie avoided Caleb's favorite breakfast food—one that she'd always enjoyed, too—because eating it conjured memories of happy mornings with him?

"Mom cried last night," the boy said matter-of-factly while taking milk from the fridge.

"Oh?" Though a part of Caleb was perversely glad she'd cried, most of him just felt sad. Not only for the years he'd missed with his son, but also with each other. They'd had a good thing going until she'd thrown it away.

"I went and asked her what's wrong, but she said nothin'. I think she's scared about the bad guys. Anyway, she let me sleep with her. I like her bed. It's bigger than mine and real squishy."

"Squishy?"

"Yeah, you know." Dowsing his cereal, Cal managed to spill a good cup of milk on the counter. When it dribbled over the edge, Caleb jumped in to help, grabbing a dish towel from the sink. "Squishy. Like bunches of pillows and stuff. Thanks for helpin' clean. Mom likes a clean house."

"I know," Caleb said.

"How?"

"Um—" Geez, where did he start?

"Caleb's an old friend," Allie said, standing in the kitchen's shadowy doorway, long blond hair a mess, eyes red and swollen. She wore a utilitarian white terry cloth robe. A yellow duck was the only decoration. He sat over her right breast. Directly over the tender patch of skin Caleb used to—no. He wasn't going there. So he dropped his gaze to her bare feet and red-tipped toes. How many times had he painted them for her?

"Where'd you meet him?" his son asked.

"School," Allie said.

"Elementary?" Cal asked.

"College."

"Oh." Cal's interest returned to cereal. Mouth full, he asked, "Hey, can we go toy shopping today? Oh— and then let's go see that new movie, *Power Force*. Sam says it's awesome!"

"Sorry, but—" Caleb and Allie both spoke at the same time.

"Go ahead," Allie said.

"You're his mother." Caleb loaded his voice with messages only she'd hear. *I'm just his father. Don't mind me.*

"Sorry, baby." She planted a kiss on the boy's forehead. "But until this trial's over, I'm afraid you'll have to stay inside, and out of public places."

"But can I at least go to school?"

"No," Caleb said.

Having expected him to argue with her, Allie had been on the verge of aiming a "stop interfering" stare at Caleb. Knowing they were on the same team—at least as far as keeping Cal safe—cocooned her in a surprising calm.

"Aw, man," Cal whined.

"I'll make you a promise, though," Caleb said to the boy, putting Allie back on full alert.

"What?" her son asked, expression once again bright.

"As soon as this trial is over, and we know that you

and your mom are safe, not only can you go back to school, but me and a team of other marshals will go with you for a while, just in case."

"Really?!" Cal asked. "And will they have guns and everything?"

"Absolutely."

"Awesome!" The boy leapt from his tall counter stool. "I can't wait to tell Sam and Reider!" He raced up the back staircase, presumably to his room.

"Thank you," Allie said.

"For what?" Caleb asked.

"Getting his mind off the depressing present and onto better times to come."

"Will times be better, Allie? Now that your secret's out, you can't expect me to just fade into the background."

After scooping ground coffee into an automatic drip filter, she shot him a look. "You know what I mean. Cal returning to school. To his normal way of life. It'll be better. I wasn't referring to us—you." Allie silently stared at the dripping coffee, trying to let the rich aroma and happy gurgle calm her jangled nerves. *Trying,* but failing. "Obviously, I don't have a clue what's going to happen between us, Caleb. Do you?"

For the longest time, her gaze locked with his. Neither speaking, breathing. And then, just when she'd thought he might be on the verge of saying something—anything— he shoved his hands in his pockets and walked away.

THAT AFTERNOON, the tension in Allie's courtroom was unbearable.

As was the heat.

The accused, Francis William Ashford, sat grinning at her, as if he'd never been charged with blowing up a post office and killing the three clerks and five customers inside—one an infant. In her two years on the bench, Allie had presided over many cases, but this one topped them all.

The gallery was filled with what had begun to feel like every reporter in the state, along with every citizen. Many used the folded take-out menu from the Chinese restaurant down the street for a fan.

Caleb, along with the rest of his six-man crew, stood vigilant watch over the crowded courtroom, occasionally speaking into microphones hidden in their suit coat sleeves.

Her current task was hard enough. And Caleb's surprise appearance had made her time off the bench insanely complicated. Still, what she was going through was nothing compared to the pain of the grieving victims' families here in the courtroom.

The prosecution asked the latest witness, a wiry, elderly black man who'd lived across the street from the post office for the past forty-two years, "Sir, could you please tell the court what you observed the morning of the bombing."

The witness cleared his throat. "I was watching my shows. *Price is Right* and the like, when I went to the front window to draw the curtain. That time of morning, sun shines right through. Produces a glare."

"Yes, sir, and did you see something suspicious?" asked the chief prosecuting attorney.

"Objection!" the defense attorney shouted. "Leading the witness."

"Overruled." To the clearly shaken witness, Allie said, "Please, Mr. Foster, continue."

"All right, well, Bob Barker had just started the second Showcase Showdown. I was pulling the curtain closed, when I saw this primer-gray truck pull up to the post office. Ford. Powerful dirty. Mud splatters all over. Had those big, oversized tires. A confederate flag hanging in the back window."

"Did the flag shock you?"

"Objection! Leading."

Allie, in no mood for attorney jockeying, shot Mack Bennett, lead attorney for the defense, her most stern look. "One more outburst, Mr. Bennett, and you will be fined. Mr. Foster, please, go on."

"All right, well, that boy—"

"Excuse me," the prosecution said, "but which *boy?* Is he here? In the courtroom today?"

"Yessir."

"Would you be so kind as to point him out?"

"I'd rather not."

"Why's that?"

"He'll shoot me."

The courtroom erupted in low rumbles.

"Order!" Allie slammed her gavel.

"Mr. Foster," the prosecution said once the crowd quieted. "Rest assured, in the county jail, the defendant has no access to firearms."

"Not him I'm worried about."

"Then who?"

"His friends. Everyone in town knows Francis has *lots* of friends living on that compound of his, and every danged one of them have *lots* of guns."

The accused jumped to his feet. "That's a bald-faced lie. I ain't never—"

"Order!" Allie said when the gallery exploded again. "Mr. Bennett, control your client or I'll have him removed!"

"Shut up, you commie bitch!" From out of the gallery someone flung an object. A balloon?

By the time she'd registered what'd happened, the courtroom had erupted in screams. Caleb and another marshal ushered Allie out of a scene that could only be described as chaos.

In her chambers, trembling, she put her hands to her face. Something wet and warm coated her cheeks. She pulled her hands down to find her palms stained with...blood?

"Hurry," Caleb said, tugging Allie's ashen-faced secretary and clerks into her office, then dead-bolting the door. He shut the drapes, then barked directions into the radio in his sleeve. "Everyone okay?" he finally asked the women assembled.

Allie nodded while her secretary fussed over wiping the blood with a tissue.

"Excellent," Caleb said. "Looks like everyone in the courtroom's all right, too. They've all been cleared. Francis is headed to his cell, and I've got a cleaning crew on the way."

"Cal?" She was almost afraid to ask.

"Just called his detail. All's clear. Per his teacher's

instructions, they're at the kitchen table practicing mul-
tiplication by making macaroni necklaces." Caleb shot
her a grin. A wonderfully sweet, strong grin so out of
place in their current situation, it made her burst into a
relieved nervous laugh.

"I—I'm sorry," she said. "I just—wow. That was—"

She was still-rambling when Caleb pulled her into
his arms. Impossibly strong, capable arms. How long
had it been since she'd been held? Since she'd had
someone to lean on? Yet as good as leaning on Caleb
felt, she couldn't open herself to the hurt of falling for
him again. It would be all too easy, losing herself in the
good. Forgetting the bad.

"S-sorry," she said. Releasing him. Backing away.
Trying hard to look anywhere but at his face. Only that
tactic landed her gaze squarely on his chest. On the rumpled white shirt he'd worn under his suit, now covered
in blood. If she'd needed a sign to warn her to steer clear
of the man she'd once loved, this was it in blazing neon.

Sure, this time the blood was part of a sick prank.

But what if next time, it was for real? What if her
worst fears about Caleb being shot came true?

Somehow she managed to say, "I—I should clean up."

Movements stiff and robotic, Allie locked herself in
her small, private bathroom. Washed her hands and
face, then sat on the closed toilet and prayed blood-
balloons were the worst of Francis's friends' arsenal.

"GOOD," CALEB SAID late that afternoon from the courthouse parking lot, hand lightly shaking as he held his
cell up to his right ear. "I caught you."

"Caleb?" his sister, Gillian, asked. "What's up? I thought you were on assignment?"

"I am."

"You got a cold?" she asked. "You sound weepy."

"Weepy?" He hadn't cried in like…a day? Just the previous afternoon, upon his first sight of his son, hadn't he spouted like a sprinkler? "I'm, ah, outside. It's damned cold."

"Cut the whole defensive tough-guy routine," Gillian said, "and just tell me what's wrong. I thought over the past year or so we've gotten further than this. You know, like we could talk."

"We can," he said. "Which is why I called. Gil, you sitting?"

"No. But I can be. Just let me put the baby down for her nap. I'll be right back."

"'Kay."

In rapidly fading daylight, drumming his fingers on the hood of his SUV, he grinned at the sound of his six-year-old stepniece's cartoons blaring over the phone.

A few years back, his sister married a great guy, Joe. The marriage turned out to be healing not just for Joe, but also for Gillian, who'd carried a chip on her shoulder the whole of her adult life.

Caleb's sister had never bothered to say anything to either her three brothers or their dad. He guessed she'd always felt as if they didn't believe she could accomplish anything other than being a classic girly girl, and the men in her family went out of their way to shelter her. Or were condescending because she wasn't their equal.

What they all knew was that hell no, she wasn't their

equal. She was better than any of them! Tougher, smarter, with a forked tongue a guy didn't stand a chance of winning an argument against!

Good thing for them, since finally figuring out all of that for herself, she'd mellowed. Taken time from her crazed agenda of proving herself better than the guys to instead learn to appreciate her own unique feminine strengths and weaknesses.

"Hi, Uncle Caleb," six-year-old Meggie said into the phone.

"Hey, potato bug."

"I'm not a bug," the girl said with giggle.

"Then what are those things sticking out of your head? I thought those were your antennae?"

"Those are my ears!" she shrieked.

"Oh, well, in that case," Caleb said, "maybe instead of a bug, you're just a Mr. Potato Head?"

"I'm a girl! I'd be a Missus Potato Head!"

"You sure? Let me ask your momma. You might be an imposter, and I'll have to call the police."

She giggled again. "You *are* the police!"

"Gimme that phone," Gillian said in the background. "You big sneak."

Giggling shrieks said his favorite little potato bug was getting tickled.

"All right," Gillian said. "I'm back. The baby's hopefully asleep, and your niece is getting popcorn crumbs all over my new sofa."

"What was that?" Caleb asked. "My tomboy sister's feeling protective toward a sofa?"

"Hey, cut me some slack. It's a really comfy sofa. Perfect for making out on."

"Ack." He clutched his chest. "I don't want to hear this."

"Hear it? Just wait till Thanksgiving when you'll get to see it. Think you'll be done in time? We're doing turkey and a ham. Dad and Beau are coming. Joe's former in-laws, too. I'm assuming you'll be holding Adam hostage?"

Caleb sighed. Rubbed his forehead.

"Out with it, sweetie. Here I am going on about the holidays when something's obviously bugging you."

"All right, here goes. Remember Allie?"

"The girl who broke your heart?"

"Aw, geez, it wasn't all that bad."

"The hell it wasn't. Adam said you didn't get out of bed for two weeks. He also said she was pregnant, then told you in a letter she'd lost the baby after leaving town."

"Adam's got a big mouth," Caleb said. "Anyway, the short of it is, she didn't really lose the baby."

"What?!"

"Gilly, I've got a son. He's so damned handsome it hurts to look at him. He's got my eyes."

"God, I'd like to hug you right now. Congratulations, honey. I can't wait to tell Dad—and Joe. I've got to see if he can wrangle time away from the office, then we'll be right over."

"Not a good plan."

She laughed. "Just try keeping me away. I love staying home with Chrissy, but truthfully, I could use a little action."

"Yeah, well, there's too much action here. And Allie and my son are at the heart of it."

"MOM," CAL SAID at the dinner table that night, "I wish you'd let me go back to school. Sam called and said Kelly got her noodle necklace stuck up her nose. And then Miz Talbert came over to try yanking it out, and then the whole thing broke, and noodles were like, *wham*—" he swung his left arm for emphasis, in the process dumping his chocolate milk "—everywhere. Sorry."

"It's okay," she said, sopping the mess without skipping a beat.

"Need help, ma'am?" The newest marshal assigned to protect them stepped in from the living room. She didn't know him, but he seemed nice enough. Cal seemed fascinated by his size and smooth-shaven head.

"No, but thanks," she said.

"Sure." All eight feet of him ducked back into the living room.

"You mad?" Cal asked, munching on a carrot stick.

"Not even a little bit." She tossed the milk-soaked rag in the sink, then joined him at the table.

"How come you're not sayin' anything?"

"Sorry," she said. "Guess I'm just tired."

"Then how come you're not eating? I thought Great-Grandma Beatrice's meat loaf's your favorite."

"It is. Guess I'm not all that hungry, either."

"I am." He helped himself to thirds on meat loaf and mashed potatoes, carefully steering clear of the steamed broccoli along the way.

"That's good," she said, not in the mood to lecture Cal about vegetables.

"Man," he said, mouth half-full of potatoes. "This was the crappiest day ever. At least Sam told everyone I have bodyguards. Wish that Caleb guy could've stayed here with me, but he said he had to hang out with you. Bet he was bored."

If only!

"Yeah," Allie said, sipping iced tea. "It was a pretty dull day." Nothing but a few blood-balloons whizzing through her court.

"Sorry. Wanna stay home with me in the morning? After I do my work, we can go see *Power Force*." The dear look on his face was so sincere, so hopeful, she couldn't help but smile. Then she happened to flash back to that afternoon, and how Caleb had worn the same concerned expression.

A pang ripped through her at the notion that no matter how hard she'd tried convincing herself that in her mind Cal's father was dead, he wasn't. He was alive and well and quite possibly lurking just outside the house.

"Oh, baby," she said, grabbing her son's small, sticky hand. "I would love to stay home with you, and then go to a movie, but I can't—we can't."

"How come you look like you're gonna cry again? You never have before."

"I know. There's just a lot going on that—"

"You'll understand when you get older." Caleb strolled into the kitchen. His choppy, dark hair was wet, as were the shoulders of his denim shirt. For the most part, his faded jeans were dry, kind of like her mouth once she'd finished eyeing the ridiculously gorgeous combo of his body and face. In his left hand dangled a plastic bag.

"It still rainin' outside?" Cal asked.

His father nodded. *His father*.

"Sure is," Caleb said. "Want to go outside and play?"

"Yeah!" Cal leaped from his seat. "Can I take my plastic boats?"

"Whoa," Caleb said, rubbing the boy's head. "Slow down, mister. That was a joke. It's a nasty night."

"It's nice in here," Cal said. "We've got meat loaf. Want some?"

"That depends. Is it Grandma Beatrice's recipe?"

"Yeah," Cal said. "How'd you know?"

Eyeing Allie, he shrugged. "Lucky guess."

"Man," Cal said, back in his seat. "You're good. What's in the bag?"

"This," he said, pulling out a Hershey bar the size of Cal's head.

"Cool!" Cal said. "Thanks! Can I eat it now? What else is in there?"

"You can eat part of it now," Caleb said. "And only if it's okay with your mom. As for what else is in there, that's for me to know and you to find out."

Cal made a face.

Caleb returned the look.

"Can I eat it?" Cal asked Allie.

"Sure," she said. "After dinner. You the new shift?" Allie asked Caleb.

"Nah. I went ahead and sent Bear out to the front porch, but I'm officially off for the night."

Cal asked, "Then how come you aren't at the new movie, *Power Force?* That's where I'd be goin' if I didn't have to work."

Caleb laughed, and the rich normalcy of his voice washed through Allie. "You work a lot?" he asked his boy.

"Yeah. Mom makes me take out the trash. I have to make my bed, too. And sometimes when I forget to take the trash, she yells at me and I get talked to about 'sponsibilities."

"What's so bad about that?"

"It's *hard.* You ever take out the trash? And sometimes, if it's raining, I even have to take out Miss Margaret's trash."

"Who's that?" Caleb asked Allie.

"Next-door neighbor, and a good friend. Before all this mess with Francis, we used to hang out a lot at each other's houses. I told her she's still welcome to come over, but she says you all intimidate her."

"Hmm…" The man Allie used to love rubbed his chin. A fine shadow of stubble had grown over the afternoon. Back in college, he'd sometimes shaved twice a day. And sometimes, when he'd chosen not to shave and they'd been messing around, he'd rubbed his rough cheeks on her neck or belly…. And she'd liked that feel. She'd wanted—

"You know," he said to Cal. "I think maybe once or twice your mean old mom nagged me about taking out the trash. But then I wised up and took it out before she even had to ask."

He shot a wink Allie's direction, and her heart flip-flopped.

Cal wrinkled his nose. "That still sounds like too much work." To his mom he asked, "Can I go watch TV and practice my knitting?"

"After you clear the table and put back the fridge stuff."

"Aw, man."

"Come on," Caleb said, reaching across the table for the ketchup and butter, flooding Allie with his all-male scent. "I'll help."

In a few short minutes, the job was done, leaving Cal scampering off to the den for TV, leaving Allie alone with his no-longer-smiling dad.

"He's good kid," Caleb said, joining her at the table.

"Thanks. I think so."

"But no way did I hear right in that he actually *wants* to practice knitting?"

"What's wrong with knitting? It's good for hand-eye coordination. Plus, if he ever gets a job in Alaska, he'll be able to keep himself warm."

Shaking his head, Caleb's only response was a grunt.

After a few seconds spent folding a leftover paper napkin into a ship, he asked, "Cal get good grades?"

"As and Bs."

"Any discipline problems?"

"Other than sass now and then, nothing serious."

"What'd you tell him about me?"

The hardball question came from left field. It took a second to regain her composure. "I—I told him you died."

Caleb cursed under his breath. Shook his head.

"Well?" she asked. "What was I supposed to say?"

He half smiled. "For being such a brilliant woman, you don't have a clue."

Chapter Three

"What's that supposed to mean?" Allie asked.

"Think about it. If you couldn't stomach being around me, how hard would it have been to at least share custody of our son? What did I ever do to make you pull something this cold? Christ. You know how much I wanted to be a dad one day…."

"One day," she said. "Not your junior year of law school. Not with marshal training after that. Not with endless hours of chasing bad guys and playing shoot-out till all hours of the night."

"So basically, you're saying you told Cal I died as a favor? So I wouldn't be bothered?"

"Right."

"And you actually believe that?" He pushed his chair back, putting her further on edge by standing directly behind her, rubbing her shoulders. Powerfully kneading, the way he'd always done after she'd had a hard day. "See, I'm thinking the whole thing goes deeper. Back to a little girl who lost her cop father at an impressionable age."

Despite his all-too-pleasurable strokes, Allie froze.

"Know what else I think?" he asked.

"Wh-what?"

"You didn't do this out of some saintly desire to shelter your son—*our* son—from pain. You were protecting yourself. That little girl inside was afraid that just like your old man, I'd get shot in the line of duty."

Brushing Caleb's hands from her shoulders, she said, "I should do the dishes."

"Leave 'em."

"What do you want from me?" she asked when he wouldn't let her up.

"Simple. When this trial mess is over, I want joint custody of my son."

"You've got to be kidding!" she said, angry enough now that she easily broke his grip to stand. "No matter what you think, Cal is *mine*. And I'm not good at sharing."

"You used to be," Caleb said, devastating her with a wink and a smile of pure acid.

"Stop. This is serious."

"Damned straight. Which is why, soon as I get back to Portland, I'll be meeting with my lawyer."

"Don't," she implored. "The whole legal route, it'll only upset him."

"Then what, *your honor,* in all your infinite wisdom, do you suggest?"

"You never used to be mean like this." She headed for the sink.

"You never used to keep secrets. Remember how we'd lounge in bed, talking all night about every little thing? How we'd drag ourselves to class in the morning too tired to read, let alone walk, the two miles 'cross campus. But by the time we wound up back at your place, we'd be recharged, ready to share our days."

"We were kids."

"Oh, and so now that you're all grown up, that makes it okay for you to hide the fact that I'm a dad?"

"No, I'm not saying it's okay. I'm—geez, would you please just go. It's been a really crappy day, and I need time to think. Breathe."

"Sorry." He stood behind her, not touching her, but close enough that she felt his heat. "I don't mean to come on so strong, but you have to know, I'm not walking away from this. Cal *is* going to be told, Allie. Soon. I've got a lot of time to make up for."

"Okay," she said. "You've made your point."

"And?"

"What?" She spun around, only to wish she hadn't, because facing him straight-on was infinitely harder. "What else do you want from me? To run right in there, and shout, *surprise,* Cal! Your dad's not dead. He's standing right here, wanting to take you away from me."

"That's not what I want, it's what—"

"Mom? I thought I heard yelling." Their son stood at the kitchen door.

"No yelling," Allie said, bustling to wipe down the counters. "Just screeching. I saw a spider. You know how I hate spiders."

"Yeah," Cal said to Caleb. "She does hate spiders."

"I know," Caleb said while Allie gripped the edge of the counter so hard her knuckles turned white. Why now? Why on top of everything else had Caleb had to reenter her life? Weren't a few death threats enough to deal with for one week?

"Mom, can I have some ice cream?"

"Sure, baby." She forced a smile. "What flavor?"

"I would want cookie dough, but that guy Adam ate it all."

"My brother, Adam?" Caleb laughed.

"He gonna buy us more?" Cal asked as Allie filled his bowl.

"Yeah," Caleb said, "I'll make sure he brings you at least three tubs."

"Thanks."

"You're welcome."

Once Cal was safely out of earshot back in front of the TV, Caleb said, "I'll tell my brother to stay out of your fridge."

"I don't care," Allie said. "Adam always did eat his own weight worth of food at least four or five times a day. Remember the time we slow-baked that huge ham to take to your dad's for Thanksgiving, then came home from class to find Adam had eaten half, thinking it was lunch?"

Caleb smiled at the memory, as did she. And it was nice, at least for the moment, to share one of the more pleasant parts of their past rather than their rocky future.

"We had some good times," Allie said. "Let's not ruin those."

"Who said I was trying to?"

"No one. I just—let me figure out a win-win solution for all three of us, okay?"

Brushing past her to help himself to ice cream, he said, "Great. That's all I ask." Gesturing to the sweet treat, he asked, "Want some?"

"Thanks." She gave him her first real smile of the day. "That'd be good."

"After that, how 'bout we watch TV with our boy?"

"You like *SpongeBob*?"

"I love *SpongeBob*—but I'm not knitting."

BARELY ONE commercial break into the show, Allie was out, curled into a ball at the far end of the sofa from where Caleb sat. He swallowed hard, remembering how she used to fall asleep using his shoulder or lap for a pillow.

Slipping a blanket from the sofa's back, he tossed it over her.

"Yo, Cal," he said to his son. "What's your bedtime?"

"Aw, man. It's eight-thirty, but can't I stay up just a little longer? I won't tell Mom."

"Sorry, pal. It's nearly nine and you've got school work in the morning."

"Five more minutes? I'll do an extra good job of brushing my teeth."

"Admirable negotiation skills, but no can do." Caleb stood, held out his hand. "Come on, I'll tuck you in."

"Do I get a story?"

"Still going to do an extra good job on those teeth?"

Ten minutes worth of tooth brushing and scrambling into pajamas later, Cal was all set for bed.

Caleb, chest tight, drew back his son's blue-and-red airplane sheets and comforter. Cal smelled like toothpaste and soap and kid sweat. Probably, he was supposed to have a bath, but seeing how he was still a virtual stranger to the boy, Caleb didn't figure one night without a bath would hurt.

He was still furious with Allie for keeping these simple pleasures from him all these years, yet he was also so damned grateful she hadn't lost their child. That she'd loved him to a degree she'd wanted to have his child.

She just hadn't loved him enough to raise his child *with* him.

Weary of the past, Caleb asked, "Which book do you want to hear?"

"Dr. Seuss! *Happy Birthday To You*'s my favorite."

"Mine, too." Caleb took it from a nearby bookshelf, then flicked on the airplane lamp on Cal's bedside table. "Like planes, huh?"

"Yeah. I like 'em a whole lot. I wanna be an astronaut, but Mom says I have to learn to fly planes before the space shuttle. Look up."

Caleb did, and grinned. Spread across Cal's ceiling was the Milky Way, along with a few extra planets and space ships NASA scientists probably hadn't yet discovered. "That's neat. Your mom hire someone to paint it?"

He shook his head. "She did it. She's a good drawer, huh?"

"She sure is. I never knew that about her."

"Did you ever meet my dad?"

Caleb coughed. "Let's, ah, get started on this book."

"Yeah, but did you?"

"Um…" Good grief, how was he supposed to handle this? "You know what, I did meet him, and he was a really great guy. You'd have liked him a lot."

"What'd he look like?" Cal popped upright in his bed. "We don't even have pictures."

"It's getting late. Shouldn't we get started on this book?"

"Yeah, but what'd he look like?"

"Ah, come to think of it, a lot like me." Caleb gently eased his son back to his pillow, then opened the book. "I wish we could do what they do in Katroo…"

"Hey, Caleb?" the boy interrupted not half a page into the story.

"Yeah?"

"Think we could play soccer tomorrow? In gym last week, I was picked last for teams. Billy Stubbs said 'cause I'm a wuss and can't kick or be goalie."

Billy Stubbs is going down.

"Sure, bud." It might take some furniture rearranging, but— "We'll play whatever you want. Get you so much practice Billy'll beg to be on *your* team."

Popping back up in his bed, Cal tossed his arms around Caleb's neck, giving him a fierce hug and sloppy kiss to his cheek. "Thanks. You're the best."

"Sure, kid." Fighting to speak past a throat tight with tears, Caleb said, "You're pretty cool, too."

ALLIE YAWNED, slowly waking to find herself alone in the quiet living room. Last she remembered, Sponge-Bob had been terrorizing Squidward. Where was everyone?

From upstairs came the muted sound of male laughter.
Big boy and little boy.

She groaned, pushing herself to her feet.

Upstairs, she paused a short way from Cal's open
bedroom door, listening to Caleb's rich voice as a familiar Dr. Seuss story unfolded. It was long. Much too
long for this late at night. Cal knew that. Obviously,
Caleb didn't. Still, she supposed it wouldn't hurt just
this once for her son to stay up late.

A burning ache took residence where her heart used
to live. What was she going to do? Judging by Cal's occasional giggle, he was enraptured by the guest in their
home. To find out Caleb was his father—what would
that do to him? Would her son be ecstatic? Or bitter over
what she'd done?

Why was a selfish part of her wanting Cal not to fall
in love with his father? Why was she so afraid of losing not just her son, but Caleb all over again? Lying to
him had been one of the hardest things she'd ever done,
yet she'd had to protect her son.

*You didn't do this out of some saintly desire to shel-
ter your son—our son—from pain. You were protecting
yourself.*

Sliding her fingers into the hair at her temples, Allie
groaned.

Damn him.

Damn Caleb for his uncanny knack of always knowing just what she was thinking. But that didn't change
anything.

Okay, so yes, maybe all those years ago she'd been
more terrified of forging a life with Caleb and then los-

ing him, than she'd been afraid for her unborn child. But now, seeing how attached Cal had become to his father in under twenty-four hours, how could she not be afraid of the wreckage that could quite possibly become of Cal's heart?

Look at their current situation. Dangerous as hell. Caleb could be shot and hurt—God forbid, *killed*—at any moment. Every day he actually looked forward to putting himself in danger. It didn't make sense.

And speaking of danger, the man was as charming as ever. She'd once fallen for him. Hard. Not that she fostered any current feelings for him. Just that—

"Oh, hey," Caleb said, startling her as he stepped outside Cal's room. "We didn't wake you, did we?"

"No."

"Cal asleep?"

Nodding, he chuckled. "Took him long enough. For a minute there, I thought I might have to slip him a mickey." He winked. "You, on the other hand, had no trouble falling asleep. Seeing you curled up on the sofa… It brought back memories."

"Good, I hope."

"Most."

Turning her back on him, heading to her room, she said, "Guess we should call it a day." She flicked on the overhead light—a modern chandelier.

"Nice," he said, hot on her trail, shrinking the once generously sized room. "You always did have a flair for decorating."

"Thanks." The money she'd spent had been her reward for having to sleep in there alone. The ultramodern acrylic canopy bed with its sheer white curtains was a floating cloud, complete with downy white sheets, comforter and pillows. She'd done the floor in dramatic black granite. Half the walls were white, the others bamboo-green. Aside from a few original botanical watercolors, all oversized and abstract, the room had few adornments.

Clutter made her crazy.

Not because it bothered her, but because Caleb had been renowned for his clutter, and she didn't want to be reminded of him. One look into her son's sage green eyes was painful enough.

"It is a little cold in here, though." He shot her a sexy-slow grin. "Needs paperbacks and newspapers. Definitely a few good flea market finds."

Arms crossed, she asked, "Am I in so much danger I need a marshal in my bedroom?"

He reddened, tipped an imaginary hat. "Sorry, ma'am. I forgot my manners."

"It's okay this once," she said, trying not to smile at his antics, but having a tough time. He'd always been a big fan of the old west, right down to adopting a truly awful fake cowboy accent. Guess he hadn't lost his touch. "Just don't let it happen again."

"Will do," he said with another gorgeous grin. "Seriously, you all right? You know, about this afternoon?"

She shrugged. Slipping off black leather heels, she headed for her walk-in closet, switching on the light.

From the bedroom came the swish of blinds being drawn on the wall of windows overlooking the backyard and Cascades range beyond. "You gotta be more careful," he said. "Until this whole mess is over, I recommend keeping all the curtains and blinds closed."

"Thanks." She emerged from the closet wearing white flannel pj's and her favorite white robe.

"Sure."

He reached out to her.

She flinched from his anticipated touch.

"Geez, Allie, all I was trying to do was get that chunk of hair from your collar. You know how you were always getting it stuck."

"Please, don't," she said, biting her lower lip.

"What?"

"Try ingratiating yourself by dredging up old memories. Yes, Caleb, we share a past, but that doesn't mean we share a future."

He snorted. "Ah, hate to interrupt your pretty speech, but there's a boy in there with my DNA who sorta says different. Our futures are intimately entwined."

"You're not playing fair." She gripped the clear acrylic bedpost, squeezing till the square edge dug into her palm. "No one's denying Cal's your son. All I asked for was time to digest all this. You showing up here out of the blue."

"Oh—like nine years hasn't already been long enough for you to devise a way to tell a son obviously needing a dad that he just so happens to have one?"

"What are you intimating? That I'm a bad mom?"

"Not at all. Just that you're *not* a dad. Did you know your expert knitter's being made fun of at school because he's lousy at sports? When's the last time you had him out playing catch or at a batting cage?"

"Stop," she said. "You're coming across like a sexist pig. Besides knitting, Cal takes art lessons. He's a highly skilled artist for his age. His teacher's quite impressed."

"Great." Caleb laughed. "Tell that to Billy Stubbs. He'll beat our poor kid to a pulp." Shaking his head, Caleb left the room.

"What's that supposed to mean?" Allie whisper-shouted, chasing him down the hall and stairs. "And who's Billy Stubbs?"

"Ask your son."

WELL, OBVIOUSLY, Allie wasn't going to wake Cal to ask, so she'd planned on asking first thing in the morning. But a storm and power outage during the night had messed up her alarm and she'd overslept, leaving her with barely enough time to ask Cal what he wanted for breakfast, let alone who this Billy Stubbs was!

And could someone please tell her, with six grown, highly capable men outside, all knowing the court schedule, how not a one of them had delivered a wake-up call?

As if being late wasn't bad enough, first thing she encountered on the kitchen counter was the plastic bag Caleb had brought in last night.

A note on it said: Allie's relaxation supplies.

Curiosity piqued, she looked inside only to swallow hard. How in the world had Caleb remembered?

Her favorite way to wind down after a really tough day was with a guilty pleasure she hadn't indulged in since…

Well, since leaving him.

With reverence, she removed the jumbo bag of

mixed-flavor Jolly Rancher candies and a movie-star gossip magazine. She sniffed the bag. Her favorite green apple flavor shone through.

Running her hand over the magazine's glossy cover, she drooled over Catherine Zeta-Jones's latest premiere gown—stunning. She snuck a quick peek inside....

Aw, Gwyneth's baby, Apple, is adorable.

Mmm…could Jude Law be any hotter?

Could Caleb be any sweeter?

Cal bounded down the stairs. "Mom? What're you doin'? It's time for us to go." He'd been so bored at the house by himself the day before, that today she'd decided to take him with her to the office. At least there, with her mostly female staff fussing over him, he wouldn't lack for attention.

"I know," she said, tucking the magazine and candy in her satchel. Just having the contraband goodies tucked beside her felt akin to taking part of Caleb to work with her—the best part. His fun side!

She was feeling good about her day ahead—how could you not feel good when gazing at Jude? Then, on the trip out of her garage past the front yard and onto the street, her day wasn't just ruined, but pulverized.

Gaping at the house, she opened her mouth to scream, but no sound came out.

How could someone have done that?

"Mom, what—"

"Look away," she said, covering Cal's eyes, glad for once to be in the back of the government-owned SUV. Why hadn't she left Cal inside, where he'd be oblivious to the malicious vandalism that'd gone on right under their noses?

On the flip side, what if he'd still be in danger inside their house, across the front porch of which someone had scrawled in blood red, *Die Commie Bitch!*

On the front steps lay the bloodied carcass of what, she didn't want to know.

"I—I thought there was round-the-clock protection?" she said to the driver. "How did those guys get so close?"

The man sighed. Rubbed his forehead. "There was a diversion, ma'am. They were in and out in a matter of seconds. Trust me, this will *never* happen again."

Allie hugged Cal close, the marshal's words offering no comfort.

Chapter Four

Upon arriving at Allie's house, fury didn't begin to describe Caleb's cold rage. "Someone mind telling me what the hell happened here last night? 'Cause unless I'm mistaken, not a damned one of you was doing your job."

Adam said, "Peterson, Juarez and Franko got sick. Food poisoning. We're guessing from that crappy convenience store on fifty-first. Old hot dogs and chili." He shuddered. "Lethal combo. Anyway, we had to call in local guys till help gets here from New Jersey."

"New freakin' Jersey?" Caleb said, eyebrows raised. "You trying to tell me the closest marshal we could get was all the way from out east?"

"Sorry, man."

"*Sorry?* That's not gonna cut it. Adam, bro, I trusted you." Lowering his voice, he said, "Allie is more than just a case to me. I mean, I'd protect any ordinary assignment with my life, but for her—" *for my son, I'd give my soul.*

"I get it," Adam said. "It won't happen again."

"It better not."

JUST WHEN ALLIE thought her current case couldn't get worse, it did. Mr. Foster, the sweet old man who lived across from the post office, was dead. The initial coroner's report said heart attack. But there were a lot of unnatural ways a so-called *natural* death could be caused.

"Ordinarily," she said from her bench, the courtroom again bursting with reporters and victims' families, "I'd want to recess in light of last night's events. But in this case, I think it'd be best for all concerned if we forge ahead."

The defense attorney launched into a showboat cross-examination leading to a series of sustained objections, during which, Francis's expression grew steadily darker.

"Damn commie bitch," the defendant eventually mumbled.

"Mr. Ashford," she said, slamming her gavel against the bench. "Congratulations. You've just earned a one-way ticket back to your cell. Bailiff."

From the gallery came a smattering of applause.

"Order," Allie said with another slam of her gavel while the defendant was escorted out of the room. When the gallery finally settled, she turned to the defense, starting to feel like the proverbial broken record. "One more stunt like that, Mr. Bennett, and you'll be fined."

The defense attorney sputtered, "But all I was doing was pointing out to the jury that my client loves to receive mail, so therefore, he couldn't have even conceived of performing a stunt so heinous, as to destroy that sainted facility from whence his beloved mail flows."

"Mr. Bennett, congratulations. You've just donated five hundred dollars to the victims' memorial fund."

The gallery erupted in still more applause—with the frequency of fines and/or courtroom removals a now regular occurrence.

By the time she'd called it quits for the afternoon session, Allie was beyond tired. With any luck, they'd be adjourned for good within a week—two at the latest.

"MOM, YOU SHOULDA' SEEN Caleb at your office today! While you were in court, he was crazy. We turned your desk around backwards and made it into a soccer goal. He got more goals than anyone ever in the whole world!"

"That's awesome, baby." Allie gave the Italian sausage and onions she was frying for spaghetti a stir.

"And then at lunch he taught me how to make a cookie Frisbee."

"And that's a good thing?" She opened a can of stewed tomatoes.

"Yeah. It was awesome. All my friends are gonna love him. 'Specially Billy."

"Who is this Billy?" Allie asked. After shaking salt on the meat, she grabbed some canned mushrooms. She'd have rather used fresh, but in light of all the recent excitement, she hadn't exactly had time for shopping. "I've never heard you talk about him."

"I dunno." From his seat at the table where he was writing his weekly spelling words, Cal shrugged. "He's just a kid in my class."

"He's been bugging you?"

"No."

Great. Now what? Violate the confidence Cal had placed in Caleb by telling her son his private conversation had been shared?

"Dinner almost ready?" Cal asked. "I'm starved."

"Almost. Just have to drain the meat and—"

"Caleb!" Cal tossed down his pencil, leaped from his chair and ran across the room, tossing his arms around his father's waist. "I had fun with you today! Wanna stay for dinner? What's in the bag?"

"Slow down, man," Caleb said, ruffling the boy's hair. "First off, there's a little something I picked up for you and your mom."

"Mom?" Cal asked. "Can I open it?"

"Sure." What was up with the curious flutter taking over her belly?

Cal ripped into the bag to pull out another memory. "Cool!" he said. "What is it?"

"A Chia Pet," Allie said, gently taking the box containing the terra-cotta Chia Man that would hopefully soon sprout green hair. Years earlier, Caleb bought her a Mr. Chia, turtle and rabbit. All lived on the kitchen windowsill of her rented house. Allie and Caleb took turns watering them. When she'd left, she'd debated whether or not to even take them. They'd been in a sense like kids. In the end, knowing Caleb's tendency to sometimes forget to water, she'd stowed them on the backseat floorboard of her Honda, where they'd gotten irrevocably mangled during a sudden stop at the intersection of Blueberry and Pine.

"Does it talk or anything?" Cal asked, suspiciously eyeing the ceramic head.

"It's a plant," she told him. "But we have to grow it ourselves."

"Oh." Cal didn't look impressed. "Thanks," he said.

Allie was already taking the head and seed packet from the box. "Thank you," she said to Caleb. "I love these things."

"I know." He stepped up behind her, creating an instant physical hum. "Whatever happened to ours?"

Nibbling her lower lip, fighting the oddest sensation that nothing between them had changed, she said, "They kind of met with an unfortunate end."

"Sounds familiar," Caleb said with a solid nod.

The flutter in her stomach died.

"Well? Can you stay for dinner?" Cal asked his father.

"Shouldn't you ask your mom first?" Caleb looked Allie's way, stealing her breath with not only his rugged good looks, but also his resemblance to her son. Correction—*their* son. Guess she might as well get used to the fact that now that Caleb knew about his child, he wasn't about to vanish from their lives, even after his team's protective services were no longer needed.

"Nah," Cal said. "She won't care. Right, Mom?" Her *darling* son flashed his most irresistible smile. Crap. The little booger knew full well she couldn't be firm when he pulled that stunt!

Even worse, Caleb flashed the same smile.

Double trouble!

"Well, Mom?" Cal asked. "Can he stay?"

"Sure. Why don't you clear your books from the table, then set three places."

"Wanna help, Caleb? We could race."

"Sounds good," Caleb said. "You start."

"'Kay."

While his son tore around clearing and setting, Caleb headed for the boy's clearly put out mother. "If it's a problem for you—you know, me staying for dinner— I can go."

"Not at all," she said, dumping the tomatoes on top of the meat so hard that little red splatters flew all the way to the stainless steel fridge.

"Sure?" He put his hand on her shoulder. For a split second, he could have sworn she'd leaned into his touch, but then the moment passed when Cal shot him with a spoon gun.

"Bang, bang! You're a bad guy and I got you!"

"Ugh—" Caleb said, grabbing his gut, groaning in serious mock pain. "The agony. It's too much."

Cal grinned. "I'm a U.S. Marshal."

"A durned good one from the looks of it," Caleb said.

"Don't," Allie said under her breath.

Cal galloped to the table with napkins and silverware.

"Don't what?" Caleb asked.

"What do you think? Encourage him to go into a dangerous profession. My god, Caleb. You've been around him a whole two days and already he's making guns from spoons."

"What's wrong with that? Girls play with dolls, boys with guns. Who knows why. That's just how it is."

"And that's supposed to make it right?"

Damn, you're beautiful. Caleb had the craziest urge to cup her cheek.

"Mom?" Cal asked, wedging himself between them. "Are we out of chocolate milk?"

"Um, I think so," she said. "Drink regular."

"I don't like it. Makes me fart."

"That's such a fibber." She landed a light swat to his behind. "Finish setting the table."

"I'm already done."

"Then wash your hands."

"Aw, Mom, I already washed 'em this morning."

"Cal," Caleb warned.

"Yes, sir." Cal scampered off to the half bath tucked beneath the stairs.

"That did *not* just happen," Allie said, grabbing the salad and slamming it on the table. "You did not just pull rank with our son. And no way did he call you, *sir*. You teach him that?"

He rolled his eyes. "A janitor loaned us an old John Wayne army flick to watch on that relic of a VCR in your office. Cal must've picked it up then."

"Caleb, please," she said, hands on her hips. "I'm serious. I see what you're trying to do. Wooing him away from me with all this manly crap. It's dirty pool."

"You get my present this morning?"

Her checks grew hot just thinking about how much she'd enjoyed reading the latest Hollywood gossip during recesses. And the Jolly Ranchers acted like fruity tranquilizers, carrying her back to a simpler time. "Yes," she said. "Thank you. But you shouldn't have done it. I ate so many green apples my teeth are going to rot out of my head."

"And what if I did this?" Caleb asked, slipping his

hands around her waist, then kissing her the way he'd wanted to since first walking into her office. Cursing the love-hate emotions for her coursing through his body. Intending the kiss to play with her, mess with her mind—just like his gift. Sure, he'd wanted to bring her a little something just to break the ice, but maybe it'd been more about wanting her to remember what a great guy she'd thrown away. How happy she'd been with him. Fun-loving and less stodgy.

His kiss was hard and claiming, the way it would've been had she been his wife. And when he was good and satisfied, certain he'd left no question in her mind as to the fact that having a man around the house was a damned good thing, he released her only to whistle his way to the stove, wishing like hell he hadn't kissed her. Praying to God and every angel he'd someday get the chance to kiss her again. "Got a colander for the noodles?"

"I can't believe you just did that," Allie hissed, lips still humming from the infuriating man's feel and taste. What she really couldn't believe was that for a second there, she'd actually enjoyed that spectacle of macho— grrr. She couldn't even begin to label what she was feeling over that stunt. "What if Cal had seen us kiss?"

"He'd have done what all kids do—said, *eeuuww*."

"Stop it, Caleb. Just stop. Stop the charm. The kisses. The gifts. It's not going to work. I'm not just going to turn my son over to you."

"Correction," he said. "He's *my* son, too. And what would it hurt for the poor kid to see his uptight mother chill?"

"Mom?" Cal said, voice small from the kitchen door. "That true? Is Caleb really my dad?"

"Oh, baby…."

"You lied!" he screamed. "You told me my dad was dead, but he wasn't. You lied! You—" He was crying so hard he couldn't talk.

When he ran up the back staircase, Allie chased after him, but Caleb held her back. "Let me," he said. "I'll smooth it over."

"Oh, like in two days you've become an expert parent? Where were you when he was up all night with colic? When he was eight months old and had a hundred-and-four fever? When he refused to go to kindergarten because he was afraid they'd make him sit next to a girl?"

"Where was I?" Caleb rammed his index finger at his chest. "*I* was back in Portland, dreaming, night after night of how things might've been if only you hadn't… Christ, the fact that you could lie about something like that. I don't know what I ever saw in you. I don't even know why I kissed you just now." He swiped his fingers through his hair. "Behold, the power of Grandma Beatrice's spaghetti sauce."

"Don't joke at a time like this."

"What else can we do, Allie? The kid's hurting. Now, you gonna keep me down here scolding me, or you want me to tackle damage control?"

"Go on," she said. "Obviously, he doesn't want to talk to me."

"He'll come around," Caleb said.

"How do you know?"

He kissed her tear-stained cheek. "I forgave you, didn't I?"

Watching Caleb mount the back stairs two at a time, Allie had to wonder how he could forgive her. Yes, her convictions for having kept Cal's father from him all these years were still strong, but while she'd spent all that time protecting her son, she hadn't stopped to consider the potential harm she might also be causing.

All this business with Billy at school was bad enough. Apparently she'd made Cal a sitting duck for schoolyard bullying. But worse than that, what had her lies done to him emotionally? How much richer might his life had been if she'd been straight with Caleb from the start?

In the same respect, how many sleepless nights would she have spent, worrying about Caleb being hurt on the job? Worrying about what kind of emotional black hole her son might fall into?

She closed stinging eyes, covered them with her hands.

If only she could've seen this coming.

But honestly, what would she have done different? Moved Cal to another state? Country? And what purpose would that have served? Sure, she might have sheltered her son for a few more years, but somewhere along the line, someway, her secret was bound to have come out.

Unfortunately for her, it'd happened now. Transforming what was already a hellish week into her worst nightmare.

"How you doin', bud?"

"Bad," Cal said, voice muffled. He sat upright on his

twin bed, cross-legged, his comforter making a tent over his small frame. "Go away. I'm sleeping."

"Okay, cool. Then I'll just sit here and talk to the dog."

"We don't have a dog," Cal said. "Mom says it hurts too bad when they die."

Caleb frowned.

Geez. Why didn't that excuse surprise him?

"Well…" Caleb said. "I suppose I could talk to the cat."

"We don't have one of those, either."

"Hamster?"

"Nope."

"Fish?"

"Caleb! Stop makin' me have to laugh, 'cause I'm really mad."

"All right, then how 'bout I just talk to this stuffed airplane?"

"Guess that'll work," Cal said.

"Okay, then here's the deal. Yeah, I'm your dad. And I gotta tell you, I'm beyond thrilled. I'm—man, there aren't even enough words to describe how much I'm loving you, and until yesterday, I didn't even know I had you."

"Really?" Cal asked.

"Would I lie?"

"Mom did." The boy sighed.

"True," Caleb admitted. "And she's sorry about that, but sometimes grown-ups lie to protect kids."

"That's stupid."

"Maybe so, but you gotta know, deep in her heart, your mom felt like she was doing her best by you."

"I'm still mad," Cal said.

"And that's okay. I'm mad, too, but you've got to work past that and look at what good came out of this."

"What?"

"What?!" Caleb tackled him, tickling the squirming laughing bundle under the covers. "You don't think having me for a dad is good?" He tickled him until the kid—his wonderful, intelligent, handsome kid—snorted.

"Quit it! I'm gonna pee my pants!"

Laughing right along with him, Caleb did quit, and after sneaking an air hole in Cal's tent, he held him and hugged him and kissed the top of his precious head right through the comforter.

I love you, I love you.

"I'm never gonna talk to Mom again. I'm only gonna talk to you. I'm even gonna live with you. And then I can have a dog and cat and rooster and donkey."

Great. Guess his speech hadn't gone quite as well as he'd thought. "Look, dude, I'm all for you living with me, and the dog and rooster sound good, but I don't know about the donkey and cat. And don't you think if you just moved out, your mom would be awfully upset?"

The human comforter tent shrugged.

"She's already cried enough the past few days, don't you think? I can't even imagine how much she'd cry if you weren't around to make her happy."

"Maybe I'll stay just a few more days. But can we go ahead and get the rooster?"

"How is he?" Allie asked from her favorite lounge chair, looking up from the dating show she'd been watching to get her mind off the horror of quite possibly being on the verge of losing her son.

"Asleep."

"But he didn't have dinner."

"He'll survive," Caleb said. "You eat?"

She shook her head.

"I'll fix us a couple plates."

"I'm not hungry."

"Yeah, well, I am and I don't like eating alone."

"Thanks," she said when he returned, handing her a plate loaded with enough spaghetti, salad and garlic toast to fill even Adam!

Caleb lowered himself onto the chair beside her. "Quite a mess we've got going here, huh?"

"It's my mess," she said, swallowing a tasteless bite of Caesar salad.

"True enough—until I went and blurted that bit about Cal being my son."

"You haven't said much about what went on upstairs. I'm taking that as a bad sign?"

"You want something to drink?" he asked. "I could grab us both milks—'course according to Cal, we might fart."

Laughing through tears pooling in her eyes, she said, "Oh god, he hates me. This was my worst fear."

"I thought your *worst* fear was having him love me, then lose me?"

She shot him a look. "You know what I mean. Having him hate me was my worst fear after my others."

"Think it's time to let go of a few of those fears?"

Stabbing a chunk of meat, twirling it with a forkful

of pasta, she said, "You don't know what it was like. Granted, you lost your mom at a pretty young age, but you at least got to say goodbye. For me," she said, dropping her fork with a clang to the plate's edge, "one minute we were planning the new built-in bookcase Dad was building in my room, and the next, he was just gone. I freaked out, Caleb. I don't think anyone but my mom and shrink know to what degree."

"I'm sorry about that, Al, but grow up. For the sake of our son, get over it. If I die tomorrow, is Cal going to be worse off for having known me? For that matter, you're not going to live forever. And no—no one connected with this case is going to get you, but god forbid, cancer could. Or fifteen gazillion other crappy diseases. Then who's going to watch over our boy? Have you even given that a thought?"

"Duh. In my will, I give Mom custody."

"Great. And she's in her sixties." Caleb roughly forked a bite of pasta and sauce. Damn Allie. His first assumption that because she'd had his child meant she obviously still had feelings for him...? Wrong! Geez, what a slap in the face to be told even if Allie died, she didn't want Cal being with his father. Total b.s. That's what that was.

He stood, then headed for the kitchen.

"Where are you going?" Allie asked, chasing after him.

"I've gotta get out of here. Your arctic chill is blowing my mind."

"But what about Cal? What do I say when he wakes up?"

"Good question," Caleb muttered. "Lucky for you, you've got a whole night to think up an answer."

Chapter Five

"Hey, Gilly," Caleb said to his sister's answering machine once he got back to his motel. "Got your message, but—"

"I'm here," his sister said, out of breath, sounding as if she'd been laughing. Glad one of them was having fun. "Sorry. Couldn't find the phone."

"Yeah, well, I don't have much to say, just getting back to you." Caleb eased his shoes off, leaning back on the lumpy mattress, conking his head on the headboard in the process. In his mind, he fired off a few dozen foul words.

"Oh. no," she said. "You're not getting off that easy. How's it going? Have you told Cal you're his dad?"

Caleb's answer was a sarcastic snort.

"Was that a good sound or bad?"

"He knows," Caleb said. "But purely by accident. He overheard me and his mom fighting about when to tell him."

"Oh, Caleb, I'm sorry. That had to be rough."

"Rough?" He laughed. "The poor kid. He's confused, Gil, and I feel so helpless. Like I just want to grab him up in a hug, but can't because he hardly knows me. And then there's his mom. She's got my head spinning."

"In a good or bad way?"

"I kissed her. Don't even know why. She was just standing there needing to be kissed."

"Could your male ego be any bigger? I mean, I'm still mad at this woman for ever hurting you in the first place, but that wasn't cool."

"I know. It's just—"

"Take a deep breath, sweetie. Cal's going to adore you. All kids do. As for his mom…" She sighed. "Sounds like you might want to back off."

ALLIE HAD SET her alarm an hour early, hoping that old adage about the way to a man's heart being through his stomach applied to little boys, as well.

By the time she was back upstairs to wake Cal to head for the office, the kitchen table was loaded with French toast, pancakes and waffles. She'd found bacon and sausage in the freezer and thawed melon and berries in lieu of fresh ones.

Her palms were sweating and her pulse hammered faster than the last time she'd worked out.

What was Cal going to say to her? Would he even talk?

"Baby," she said, perched on the edge of his bed. "Time to wake up. I made you a special breakfast."

Cal slowly came around, rubbing red eyes.

Guilt didn't begin to describe the crushing pain in her chest. She'd done that to him. Caused those tears. Sure, at the time she'd written on his birth certificate that his father was deceased, she'd felt her actions justified. In her mind, Caleb might as well have been dead.

But now… Now, she wasn't so sure.

"Come on," she said, giving her son's back a rub. "Gotta get ready for work."

"Is Caleb coming?" Cal asked.

"With you? To hang out in my office?"

He nodded.

"I don't know," she said. "Probably. Want me to find out?"

He nodded.

"Sweetie, I know you're upset with me, but—"

"Excuse me," he sat up, then scooted around her and off the bed. Had she only imagined him giving her a wide berth so as to not have to touch her? "I've gotta go to the bathroom."

"Okay," she said. "Need help picking out clothes?"

"No, thank you."

"Okay, well…."

He shut and locked the bathroom door.

"How's it going?"

Allie jumped. Put her hand to her chest. "Caleb. Wish you'd learn to knock."

"Sorry," he said, joining her at the kitchen table. "Quite a spread you've got here. This might even feed Adam."

She flashed him a weak smile, appreciating his stab at humor, but he wasn't the one who'd just lost his son.

No. He gained a son, no thanks to you.

Shame washed over her, but still she kept her chin high.

What's done is done. No matter what Cal thought of her, she was still his mother. Nothing would change that. It was her duty to protect him from a father who protected everyone under the sun except himself.

"So?" Caleb said. "How'd it go with Cal? I'm assuming he's still upstairs?"

She nodded, unable to speak past the lump in her throat.

"Want me to talk to him?"

She nodded again.

Hand over hers, he said, "He'll come around, but just for a second, put yourself in his shoes."

"I know," she said with a messy sniffle, napkin to her nose.

Caleb took the stairs two at a time.

Allie sat at the table making swirls in congealing syrup with her fork. Everyone who knew the truth about Cal's father, her closest friends and mother, told her they supported her decision, but in their eyes, Allie had seen their true opinions. That she'd been wrong to keep Cal from his father. But what did they know? They had no idea how devastated she'd been by her dad's sudden death. Right off the bat, poor Cal would've had to deal with a father whose career put him on the fast track to his grave.

How many nights during her pregnancy had she lain awake weighing her options? And despite Caleb's belief that all she'd been thinking about was her own possible pain if he'd been unexpectedly killed, she had thought about his hopes and dreams. Just because she disapproved of his career path, that didn't give her the right to impose her fears upon him. All his life Caleb had wanted to be a marshal—just like his dad.

It was a sickness. In his blood.

True, she could have begged him to put aside those dreams. Asked him for the sake of their baby, for her, to become something safe, like an accountant. But realistically, how long would their marriage have lasted? Caleb would've been miserable. She couldn't have done that to him. She couldn't have let her fears steal his dreams.

"Allie?" Caleb said. "How about fixing this hungry boy a plate?"

She looked up.

Caleb led their son down the stairs.

Cal had a death grip on his dad's big hand.

"Want a little of everything?" she asked their son.

As if he couldn't bear to look at her, he stumbled into his usual chair, then nodded.

Caleb, drawing out the chair beside Cal, flashed her a sympathetic look, but she could well imagine what he was thinking.

You reap what you sow.

"How about thanking your mom for this great spread?" Caleb asked, slathering butter on his pancakes.

"Thanks, Mom."

"You're welcome, baby. Want some juice? Hot chocolate?"

He shook his head.

Cautious morning sun snuck past the shuttered windows, lending the usual cheerful kitchen the feel of a cave. As if she were stuck deep inside, when just a few feet away was freedom. Her old, happy way of life. She resented Caleb for even being here, yet in the same breath was thankful to him for at least trying to smooth the way for her with their son.

Caleb said, "Heard you had to boot Francis from the courtroom yesterday. Think he'll give you trouble again today?"

"Who knows." *Who cares.* All she could think about was the damage she'd done to her son.

"Cal," Caleb said while reaching for the platter of bacon. "You tell your mom about your soccer goal yesterday?"

"I forgot."

"You forgot? Buddy, it was awesome! The way you handled that ball—once you show those skills of yours out in public, I wouldn't be surprised if scouts pulled you from third grade to make you go pro."

"Really?" His smile lit his whole face. "That'd be awesome."

"Except for one thing," Allie said. "I'd miss you."

"Dad could go with me on the road," Cal said. "You could stay here. By yourself."

"I, ah—" Allie pointed toward the stairs. "Better get ready for work." Pushing back her chair, she took off at a dead run, before the dam of tears broke.

"Allie, wait," Caleb called out. "He didn't mean it."

"Yes, I did," Cal spat. "I *hate* you, Mom. You're a liar! I only love Dad!"

"ALLIE, HON," Caleb said. "Please stop crying. He's just eight. Half the time I'm sure he doesn't know what he's saying." Caleb had found her in her bedroom, sobbing her eyes out while their son gorged himself on the waffles and pancakes and breakfast meats she'd undoubtedly been up preparing since dawn.

"Y-yes, he does," she said with a sniffle. "He's right. I'm a horrible mom. I've been lying to him his whole life. And what's wrong with me? I never cry, but lately, I can't stop. I'm always strong and in control, but now… I'm horrible on multiple levels."

He pulled her into an awkward hug, wishing her every curve didn't still fit him like a glove. "You're not horrible, just confused. On a lot of issues—especially my job. Damn, Al, you seem to think I'm some Rambo out there with guns blazin'. But it's not that way. Most days, I'm in my office, chasing paper trails. And even on days I am doing dangerous work, I've got equipment and procedures that your father never had to keep me safe."

She drew back, snorted and nodded. "I'm sorry," she said, pushing at her hair. "I've got to pull myself together. I'm due in court in twenty minutes."

"Want me to get you out of it? Cite personal safety?"

She shook her head. "Thanks, but that'd just be delaying the inevitable. I'd just as soon get this one over with."

"Cal's going to come around, you know. No kid I've ever hung with stayed mad long."

Her master bath was partially open to the rest of the room, and he just stood there like a goon, watching her brush her long, blond hair into a stark, professional ponytail, watching her apply sheer coats of eye shadow and mascara. She wore her white flannel pj's and big, white robe. Even now, with her makeup on and hair polished, she had a vulnerability about her sucking him in. He wanted to protect her, hold her, hug her, make everything better.

But why?

The woman had destroyed him.

It'd taken years to recover emotionally—if he ever had. To find out she'd had the audacity to keep Cal from him all these years—it was the cherry on the cake leading to a forever kind of splitsville.

No matter how beautiful she still was, or how much she seemed to need him, the two of them, together again as a couple? That wasn't going to happen.

Now, he and his son, that was a whole different story.

Caleb would have partial custody. Might be a bear to hammer out the terms, but he and Allie were two reasonably intelligent adults. Between them, they could figure out an equitable split.

While he'd been lost in thought, she'd ducked into her closet and shut the door. She now emerged. All business in a sleek black suit. "Guess if you're ready to take me, I'm…" That last word seemed stuck in her throat.

"Um, great," Caleb said. "Let me alert the team and we're good to go."

"YOU OKAY?" Adam helped himself to the stash of Jolly Ranchers Allie now kept in a crystal bowl on her office desk.

"Depends on your definition of okay." They were on lunch recess, and after a tense morning of expert forensic testimony, she doubted she'd be able to eat a thing.

Still, a long afternoon of testimony loomed ahead, so if she didn't grab a bite now, she'd be out of luck till dinner.

"Well," Adam said, crunching his candy, "you haven't been shot at lately. That's a good thing. And hey, any day spent without my grumpy-ass brother is a good day."

"He's been testy?"

"As a bull in line for castration."

She winced. "Love you, Adam. You always have had a way with words."

"Any idea what bug flew up his butt?"

"He hasn't told you?" she asked, raising her eyebrows while sinking her teeth into her dry ham sandwich.

"Obviously not." Snatching the bundle of grapes from her lunch, he asked, "Can I have these?"

"Sure."

"So?" He put his feet on her desk. "What's up between you and my brother?"

She took another bite of sandwich, wishing she had globbed on about a gallon of mayonnaise to help it go down. "You should probably let him tell you."

"Ha! That'll be the day. He never tells me a thing except what I do wrong."

"I thought you two had a great relationship?"

He shrugged. "Used to. 'Bout the time you two split, it went sour. He's been all work, and not much play."

"So he hasn't dated much?"

"Try never—well, except for a waitress down at the I-5 Waffle Hut. But I don't think they ever got serious."

He popped a grape. "Last I heard she married a truck driver. Caleb wasn't too busted up. How 'bout you? Date much?"

She laughed. "No time."

He rolled his eyes. "You must've had time somewhere along the line. How else did you get—" He stopped talking long enough to count on his fingers. "Whoa. No wonder my brother's pissed. Not cool, Allie. Not cool at all." He lowered his feet. Tossed what was left of her grapes back on her flattened paper bag. "I'll be outside when you're ready to head back in."

"Adam, wait. Let me expla—" What was it about the Logue men that constantly had her playing catch-up?

Why did she even care?

Why? Because her and Adam had always been buddies. That condemning look he'd just given her hurt. It was the same look she'd seen on Cal and Caleb and her mother and even her good friend and neighbor, Margaret. And dammit, she didn't want to see it again.

She was tired of being judged.

Yes, she'd made a not very popular decision, but Cal was her son. As his mother, she'd had to do what she believed was in his best interest. At his birth, keeping him from a father who played Wild, Wild West for a living had seemed like a very good thing.

In retrospect, maybe she hadn't thought the whole plan through. Maybe she should've planned for a contingency like this. But back then, all she'd had to go on was her gut feeling. The one screaming that Caleb's job was reckless and inconsiderate and selfish.

Yeah, but if he's so selfish, then why's he here, putting his life on the line for you and your son?

Rubbing her forehead, Allie closed her eyes and sighed.

"MS. SMITHSON," the prosecution asked during the afternoon session. "Could you please tell the court what you observed the morning of the bombing?"

"Well…" The middle-aged, strawberry-blonde hesitated before answering, darting glances toward the jury, then back to Francis. "I was out watering. We'd had a bit of a dry spell. I was just coiling up the hose when I noticed a gray pickup slowly approach the post office. I thought it was odd—the way it just stopped at the door instead of pulling into a space. Loretta—the Postmaster, bless her soul—she frowned on that sorta thing seeing how one car in the lane blocked the whole lot. She always said it wasn't near big enough to accommodate all the traffic.

"I was just about to call the sheriff on account of that truck just sittin' there, clogging everything. Alice Beasley pulled up behind, honking and honking her horn, which got my little dog, Cocoa, all wound up. Next thing I knew, Francis was jumping out of the truck, running and running just as fast as he could. Alice kept honking, then started shouting out the window, and then, bam! The whole thing just blew."

"Just the truck?"

"No. *Everything*. The truck. Post office. Poor Alice. It was like the whole world was on fire." Shaking her head, she said, "I've never seen anything like it. Scared me half to death."

"Thank you, Ms. Smithson. Now, just one more thing. You sure you got a good look at the man running from the truck?"

"Yessir. It was him." She pointed to the defendant. "Francis William Ashford."

The gallery went nuts. Allie slammed her gavel, but it didn't help. "Order!"

Finally, the crowd quieted down. The prosecuting attorney thanked Ms. Smithson for her testimony. The defense had a short, bumbling rally with her, then excused her from the witness chair.

The heavyset woman let the bailiff take her arm. On her way out the room's rear exit, she shot a worried glance over her shoulder.

Allie said a quick prayer for the witness's safety. Testifying against Francis had been a very brave thing.

If only Allie had had the same kind of courage nine years earlier when she'd first told Caleb she was pregnant. Maybe then everyone wouldn't now be hating her—including her son.

Chapter Six

"Sorry, bud," Caleb said to his son the next morning, Allie was still upstairs, getting ready for her day. "But with all that's been going on lately, I'd still feel better with you hanging out here at home, or at your mom's office."

"That's not fair," Cal said, slamming his red backpack on the kitchen floor. "I'm bored. All this is Mom's fault. If she wasn't so mean to everyone in court, they wouldn't—"

"Whoa." Caleb yanked his son back by his shirt collar. "Don't *ever* say something like that about your mom. What she does is important. She doesn't hurt people, she helps them by making sure bad guys like the one who blew up the post office and shot at you get sent to jail for a very long time."

"I don't care," Cal said. "I hate her, and now I hate you, too, 'cause you're yellin' at me. My real dad wouldn't ever yell. He loves me. You're just some fake dad! I wish I'd never even seen you!"

While Cal raced up the stairs, crying all the way, Caleb parked on a bar stool, turning his own hate on his boss, Franks. All of this was somehow directly his fault. For had Caleb been given a choice, there was no way in hell he'd have voluntarily gotten messed up with Allie again.

But wait. If he hadn't had to suffer through seeing her, he never would've met his son. And no matter how upset the little guy was with him at the moment, Caleb could take the heat. No matter what Cal thought, Caleb knew damned well he was his real dad by blood.

Now, the trick was to start being his real dad by actions.

Starting with sucking down his wounded male pride and taking care of business he'd started some nine years earlier.

Taking the stairs two at a time, he ignored the obnoxious pop music blaring from his son's room, and headed toward the opposite end of the hall.

His first inclination was to storm through Allie's closed bedroom door. But in light of the question he'd come up here needing to ask, maybe it'd be best if he adopted a gentlemanly technique.

Knocking, he called out, "Allie?"

Her answer was to switch on the blow dryer.

At the other end of the hall the noise level went down, then came the click of an opening door. Cal stuck his head out. "Thought you left."

"Nope."

"But I told you to," Cal said.

"And you think that's going to make me go?"

Cal shrugged.

"How long's it usually take your mom to dry her hair?"

"Forever."

Caleb sighed. "That's what I remember, too."

Cal stepped one foot outside his room, but kept his hand on the doorknob. "How come you know so much about my mom? I mean, I know you guys were friends in college and stuff, but I don't know how long it takes my friend Clara to dry her hair."

"Long story, bud." Caleb sighed. "Let's just say we were a little more than friends."

"Like she was your girlfriend?" Cal made a face akin to having his mouth full of brussel sprouts and worms. *"Eeeuuw."*

"Be careful," Caleb said. "One of these days you just might find a girl you like, too."

"Nuh-uh. Girls stink."

Allie's hair dryer went quiet.

"She's done," Cal said.

"Yep." Caleb slipped his hands in his pockets.

"Well? What'd you wanna talk to Mom about? You gonna tell on me?"

"Nope."

"Really?" The boy's eyebrows shot up.

"You think there's something I should tell her?"

He touched his chin to his chest.

"Look," Caleb said, crossing to Cal's end of the hall. "What happened downstairs—it's between me and you, 'kay?"

"I wasn't very nice."

"You've had a lot to get used to in the past few days. We all have. Guess I haven't been feeling very nice, either."

Cal peeked up. "Can I go to school?"

"Nope."

"Please?"

"Not a chance," Caleb said.

"When are you gonna catch those bad guys?"

"Soon as possible."

"Then I can go to school?" Cal asked.

"Yep."

Cal threw his arms around Caleb's waist, nearly toppling him with the force of his hug. "Sorry," he said.

"Me, too."

"Yeah, but you didn't say mean stuff."

Allie's door creaked open. "How come I wasn't invited?" she said.

"To what?" Cal asked.

"The party." She looked cool and professional with her long hair smoothed into a ponytail, her curves downplayed by a severe black pantsuit.

A few minutes earlier, Caleb had been one hundred percent clear on his mission. Now he wasn't. What if he told Allie it was high time they got married and she flat refused? What if he stood there feeling and looking like a damned fool, yet he still wasn't any closer to sharing custody of his son? Even worse, what if she followed a page from her past by pulling another vanishing act?

"You look good," Caleb said.

She flashed a faint smile. "If you were Francis, would you be scared of me?"

"Oh, hell yeah," he said, forgetting his munchkin audience. "Sorry," he added for Cal's grinning benefit.

"That's okay," the boy said. "Billy says way worse words than that all the time at recess."

"Great," Caleb said, shaking his head at his son's admission.

"Remind me when this trial is over," Allie said, "to schedule a meeting with your teacher." To Caleb she said, "Should Cal stay here today, or go with me to the office?"

"I've already sent one of my men to get his assignments for the rest of week," Caleb said. "Then I'd feel better keeping him with us. Keeps my crew more concentrated."

"Sounds logical," she said with an efficient nod. "Okay, then, let me grab a coffee and granola bar and we're good to go. Cal, you already eat cereal?"

The boy nodded.

Caleb opened his mouth to tell her about his plan for them to marry, but no sound came out. Yeah, he wanted to wake up to this amazing little boy's hugs every day, but what about Allie? Marriage implied a helluva lot more than just being a dad.

There were logistics to be worked out. *Big* logistics.

All stuff he could handle later.

Much later.

Like maybe tomorrow.

Even better, the day after.

"Dad?" Cal asked, already heading down the back staircase. "Didn't you need to talk to Mom?"

"No," Caleb said, gesturing for Allie to led the way.

She glanced at her watch. "I'm not due in court till nine. What's up?"

"Nothing. It'll wait."

She brushed past him, flooding his senses with her feminine smell. Pretty shampoo and soap supercharged by her heat. "It's okay. Really, I've got time."

He closed his eyes and swallowed.

What was he going to do? Granted, he would ask her to marry him, but shouldn't he try pizazzing the moment? Maybe beg a favor from one of the off-duty guys to at least grab some flowers?

"Caleb?" She blocked his way, brushing the backs of her fingers against his forehead. "You feeling okay?"

"Ms. HINSHAW," Francis's attorney said to the elderly woman on the witness stand—another in a long line of neighbors to the usually peaceful Limon Street Post Office Francis William Ashford was accused of having blown up. "I know this must be exhausting for you, but bear with me just a few minutes more. Now, I realize you've already been over this in a roundabout way with the prosecution, but for the benefit of the record, could you please tell me what you witnessed the morning of the supposed crime."

Arthritic hands trembling, she reached for the water glass that sat on the witness stand rail. She took a slow sip before carefully setting the glass back down, then clearing her throat.

"Ms. Hinshaw," the attorney said, "I don't mean to rush you, but whenever you're ready."

She glanced at Francis, then to her hands clenched on her lap. "I didn't see anything. I don't even know why those people brought me in here." She pointed to the glaring prosecuting attorneys.

Murmurs filled the gallery, and for the umpteenth time since the trial's start, Allie slammed her gavel.

"Ms. Hinshaw," Allie said, "I have to ask, has anyone, in any way, threatened you if you testify against Mr. Ashford?"

"Of course not," the woman said, her gaze darting everywhere but to Allie. "What kind of person do you think I am?"

A scared person.

"WHILE CAL'S still in your office," Caleb said to Allie while she was on a court recess three days later, "I'd like to run something past you."

"Sure," Allie said. They stood in the secure hall leading from the courtroom to her chambers. With Caleb mere inches away, smelling far too yummy for comfort and wearing a suit with a crumpled white shirt she had an insane urge to hand press the wrinkles from, standing around gabbing was a danger to her emotional well-being. Still, she asked, "What's up?"

"You know my sister, right? Gillian?"

"Sure."

"Well…" Caleb scratched his head. "Gil got married a few years back, and ever since then, she's turned into this bizarre cross between Rambo and Mother Goose."

Allie grinned. "Don't tell me she went into the family business? She a marshal, too?"

"Yes, ma'am. Currently on extended leave. So anyway, she married a great guy, Joe, who already had a great little girl, Meghan. They also have a baby of their own, Chrissy. Makes for big fun around the holidays."

"How wonderful," Allie said, squelching the pang ripping through her upon the realization that along with keeping Cal from his father all these years, she'd also kept him from family. Cousins and aunts and uncles. A grandfather.

"Yeah, well," Caleb said, "I used to think so, too, but then I made the mistake of letting her in on our secret."

"You mean about Cal?"

He nodded.

"And…" She waved him on.

"She, and ah, my dad and the rest of the gang want to meet him. *Now*."

"Oh." Another pang came along with wondering where she'd fit in to the meet-and-greet. Cal was their blood relative. She was only the woman who'd kept him from them all those years.

Caleb said, "I was thinking once the trial wraps up, we could do something special. Invite my family. Get that first meeting over with."

Get it over with?

Allie took a deep breath and counted to ten.

Was it just her, or did that phrase sound eerily similar to the one he'd uttered when she'd told him she was pregnant? The one where instead of proposing to her, he'd mumbled over and over about how he'd *make it right*.

"Well?" he said, nodding toward her closed office door, behind which Cal was presumably getting his homework done. "Sound like a plan?"

"I don't know," Allie said. "Even if Francis's fate is a done deal by then, think it'll be safe? I mean, with all that's been going on around here lately, maybe it's not the best place for a little girl and baby."

He rolled his eyes. "Not only will my crew still be on duty, but my whole family, aside from Joe and the kids are marshals. We'll handle a weekend with kids just fine."

"What about that incident on the porch?" Allie asked. "You couldn't *handle* that."

"I wasn't there." He sharply looked away, then back. "If I had been, it never would've happened. So what's it gonna be, Al? Assuming the trial's over, is my family welcome?"

"It's not that easy," she said.

"What're you scared of?"

"I don't know what you mean."

"Oh, come on. You think my family's sole reason for coming over here is to drill you? Condemn you?"

"And you think they won't?"

"Who knows what they'll do. They're not my puppets, but friends. Can you blame them if they're bitter? You didn't just lie to me, Allie, but to all of them."

"I know," she said under her breath, wishing the entire issue would go away. Knowing, deep in a secret place in her heart, that to never see Caleb again would destroy her. "Do we have to go over this here? Now?"

"If not now, when? I don't like plans left up in the air."

"Soon, okay? I just need time to think." Breathe. Somewhere safely away from her crazy urge to plant her hands on his chest, eternally seeking comfort where there was none.

"Sure. Sorry to pressure you, I just—" He reached out to her, hooking his index finger with hers. The touch was so slight, it shouldn't have meant anything.

But it did. It meant everything that even though he understandably still held a grudge for her many sins against him, there was also a part of him compassionate enough to try to help her through this latest awkward patch in what'd begun to feel like an increasingly awkward life. "I want us to feel the way we used to," he said. "Like my favorite jeans and sweatshirt."

"Stop." If she hadn't laughed, she'd have cried. Fingers over his lips, she said, "Do you have any idea how many unflattering things you've said to me in the past five minutes?"

"Like what?" He captured her fingers, tucking them against the chest she'd so longed to touch. Whether he knew it or not, he'd made a mistake in placing her hand over his heart. For it'd never been able to keep a secret, and now was no different as it beat an erratic tune against her palm.

"Oh," she said. "Like I should be flattered you're comparing me to one of your ratty old sweatshirts?"

"Hey, I could've compared you to—"

"Judge Hayworth," said Giselle, one of her clerks. "Sorry to bother you, but before you head back to the bench, could I get you to sign these?"

"Sure," Allie said, taking the sheath of papers.

"Thanks," Giselle said, not hiding her curiosity about Caleb. "Well?" she asked Allie. "Aren't you going to introduce me?"

"Sorry," she said, fumbling her way through introductions. Hating herself for gritting her teeth through a handshake that went on for far too long. But was that really what Caleb was? Her friend? *Just* her friend?

"Nice to meet you," Giselle said. "If the judge here ever gives you time off for good behavior, be sure and let me know."

Allie frowned when Giselle's parting gift to Caleb was a sassy wink.

"Will do," he said, just a tad too flirty.

HOURS LATER, after a grueling afternoon in court viewing crime scene photos, Allie was loading briefs into her satchel when a knock sounded on her closed office door. Cal was safe, playing video games with Adam and three other marshals in an office down the hall.

The door opened, and Giselle popped her head through. "Judge Hayworth, do you have a second?"

"Sure," Allie said. "What's up?"

"That's what I was going to ask you." The tall, creamy-complexioned brunette walked the rest of the way into the room. She'd graduated at the top of her law school class, and spent every spare second studying for the bar. Her father was a federal judge in the state's largest district. He wanted her to gain practical experience before joining her uncle's thriving criminal defense firm in D.C.

"Here's the thing," Giselle said. "You know Mom's hosting a reception for me in Portland this weekend, and she wants me to bring a date." She rolled her eyes. "Like I really have time to date."

The sick feeling in Allie's gut told her she didn't like the direction this conversation was about to take.

"Office gossip says you and the head of your security detail have a past. But he's way hot, and I'm wondering if you all have a future? If not, is he fair game?"

Good question.

"Mom and Daddy just love salt-of-the-earth, hero types."

"Sure?" Allie was more confused than ever where her feelings stood on Caleb. The only absolute was that the mere thought of him going anywhere with the gorgeous creature standing before her, let alone on a date to meet *Daddy,* had Allie's pulse raging.

"Sure," Giselle began, "meaning *sure,* he's fair game? I don't want to step on any toes, but…" She flashed Allie a beautiful smile. Was it wrong to want to claw out Giselle's blue eyes even though Allie had no business wanting Caleb for herself?

"Actually," Allie said, slamming her desk drawer shut, "Caleb and I are sort of an item."

Giselle's eyebrows shot up. "Sort of?"

"It's complicated," Allie said.

"I'll bet."

"I HAD AN INTERESTING chat today," Allie said that night while helping Caleb prepare a salad. While she washed lettuce, he sliced tomatoes.

His gift for the day had been a giant, jewel-toned totem pole of sorts, only instead of carved images, there were hundreds of rhinestones and beads and tiny mirrors. Never would she have thought to pick it out for herself, but it looked amazing in the den. She'd squealed and hugged him—then felt guilty for lingering in his arms. For liking the feel of those strong arms even more than the gift.

"With who?" Caleb asked.

"Giselle. One of my clerks."

"She that hottie we ran into at recess?"

She flicked him with cold tap water.

"I'll take that as a yes." He grabbed a green pepper she'd already washed.

"Anyway," she said, striving to infuse an appropriate devil-may-care lightness into her tone, "looks like you have a secret admirer."

"Giselle?" His eyebrows shot up. "Cool."

"She wanted to know if you were available for escort services this weekend."

"You told her I am, didn't you?"

"That's mean," she said.

"Oh," he teased, "like you aren't being mean by keeping me hanging?"

"How have I done that? I wasn't aware we even have a topic between us to hang."

"There could be," he said. "If you wanted."

"Oh, yeah?" Standing shoulder to shoulder, hip to hip, she was having a hard time keeping up her half of the witty banter. "Like what kind of topic?"

"You need kissing," he said.

"And you need taking down a notch."

"You going to be the one to do it?"

"Maybe." They'd inched even closer, and now stood belly to belly, chest to breasts. How easy it would be for Allie to forget the past and go with the moment. Remember the way things used to be. The way she'd always dreamt they could be.

She wanted him to kiss her. Desperately.

Understanding why was out of the question when the

heat of his exhalations brushed her upper lip, teasing her, taunting her, placing her on a time machine straight back to her sweet little rented house and all the places they'd christened in their own special way.

He smoothed his hands along the curve of her hips.

She flattened her palms against his chest, wondering at the solidity. The strength. His heart wasn't racing, but was beating slow and steady.

She licked her lips and ducked her head slightly before raising it. Incapable of focusing, thinking, of anything but his mouth. His amazing, sensuous, magical—

"Mom?" Cal asked. "Is dinner almost—*eeuuw*. What're you two doin'?"

Caleb groaned.

"That was my friend Clara on the phone," Cal said. "She was tellin' me about our science fair project."

Allie pushed her fingers into her hair. When had the phone rung?

"What're you making?" Caleb asked their son.

"I'm thinking a volcano. Or seeing how long it takes for bread to grow mold."

"My sister went to the state science fair two years in a row," Caleb said, setting the salad bowl on the kitchen table.

"What'd she make?" Cal asked.

Caleb laughed. "Honestly? Don't have a clue. She's coming for Halloween, though, so you can ask her yourself."

"Really?" Cal asked. "How old is she?"

"Thirtysomething. I forget her exact age. She does have a six-year-old daughter, though. Plus, a baby girl."

"Man…" Cal shook his head. "That's an awful lot of girls."

"She has a husband, too. And you'll get to meet your granddad and another uncle."

Taking the chicken breasts from the broiler, Allie felt a little faint. Whatever happened to her being in on the decision on whether or not Gillian and her family came for a visit?

"Mom?" Cal asked. "Do you know all these people?"

"Most," she said, setting the chicken on the table.

"They nice?" he inquired.

"I always thought so," she said. "Ready to eat?"

"Guess I messed up," Caleb said out of earshot of their son. "I meant to get your okay about my family descending on your corner of the world, but guess I was so excited by the prospect, I forgot. Sorry."

She'd been all set to be angry with him, but one look at his handsome face parted by a goofy, boyish grin, and unfortunately, she was right back to wanting to kiss him! Not to mention explore more of that mystery topic he'd teased her about!

"It's okay," she said. "Guess we might as well get it over with."

"That how you really feel?" he asked, helping her gather salad dressings and the salt and pepper on the way to the table. "Like meeting my family is a hard-ship? Something not to be enjoyed, but dealt with?"

"You guys are boring," Cal said. "Can I go eat in front of *SpongeBob,* then do my knitting?"

"No," Allie said.

"Sure," Caleb said.

"Thanks, Dad!" Seeing how he held his plate in one hand, Cal gave his father a one-armed hug before dashing off to the TV.

Allie pulled out a chair at the table and all but collapsed, cradling her forehead in her hands.

This was getting out of control.

Her son's lack of discipline.

Her attraction to Caleb.

For all practical purposes, her entire life!

Caleb joined her at the table. "I'd appreciate you staving off your nervous breakdown long enough to answer my question."

"That was uncalled for," she said, nodding toward the blaring TV.

"And your trashing my family was A-OK?"

"I don't want to do this," Allie said. "I *can't* keep up this fighting. Not when I'm facing Francis every day."

"So you tell me then, Al. What do you want to do? I mean, here I sit, trying to bring us closer, but the vibe I'm getting from you is that you'd feel better if we'd have just stayed apart."

"That's not true," she said. "I never—"

He leaned in close, violating every last remaining millimeter of her personal space. "You never lied to me? Telling me you'd lost our baby, when in reality, you were healthy as a freakin' ox and planning on carrying it full term without me. Planning on raising him without me. You gonna even try denying that if I hadn't ended up in Calumet City by assignment, that you never would've searched me out?"

Jaw hardened, fingers clenched, she asked,

"What's it going to take for you to once and for all forgive me?"

"What's it gonna take?" he shot right back. "You finally marrying me. Promising to never—*ever*—run out on me again."

After all this time, after all of her hoping and praying, he'd said the "M" word. But him essentially telling her they'd be married was hardly the dreamy proposal she'd longed for. It didn't mean anything. Not really. Certainly not that he was willing to abandon his dangerous career.

She looked at him, desperately searching for something indefinable in his expression. Was he madly, deeply in love with her, only too shy to admit it?

Judging by the flinty edge to his normally warm eyes—no. This wasn't about timidity, but pride. Wounded male pride over her having run off with his son, and now, Caleb didn't want her so much as he wanted Cal.

Finding it unfathomable to stay in this kitchen—this world—with the man she'd once so deeply loved a second longer, Allie scraped back her chair and bolted up the stairs.

"Aw, hell," Caleb muttered, escaping his own chair to chase after her.

Chapter Seven

Caleb found Allie lying on her stomach on her bed, crying her eyes out.

He was the reason.

He was a jackass.

"I'm sorry," he said, climbing in beside her, spooning her as best he could. "I'm so damned sorry." When she said nothing, but had at least quieted her sobs, he said, "Do you have any idea what it did to me, Al? Going to your house—*our* house—that Friday night, only to find it empty? It didn't just hurt me, it destroyed me."

She broke his hold to roll over to face him. Her eyes were red and swollen. Her makeup a mess. And still, she was beautiful. *His.* Just as she'd always been. And if he had anything to say abut it, she would be his again.

"I've apologized for that," she said, voice wobbly and thin. "Not just to you, but your family, over and over a thousand times in my head. I was young. Stupid. Scared. Proud. I'm not saying that excuses me…my actions. Just that's how it was." She reached out to him, toying with one of the buttons on his shirt. "Back then,

I loved you so much. Maybe too much. When I found out I was carrying your child, I should have been upset and overwhelmed, but truthfully? Caleb, I was elated. All I could think of were the brilliant careers we had ahead of us. The wonderful life spent raising our little boy or girl. We could've have had so much fun, but you threw it all away."

"What the hell are you talking about?" he demanded. "I asked you to marry me."

"No—you told me you'd *make it right*. There's a huge difference."

"Bull."

"Think what you want," she said. "I saw the truth in your eyes. You *didn't* ask me to marry you, and I knew you didn't love me enough to give up your damned dangerous job. What if we had gotten married and lived happily ever after, only then you galloped off to work one day and didn't come home?"

"People die, Allie. Lawyers and bakers and—hell, I don't know. Brick layers." A muscle annoyingly ticked in his clenched jaw. "You can't live your life in fear."

"Who says?" she shrieked. "Who named you the Fear Police?"

"Fear Police?" He couldn't help but grin. And then she was grinning, too. And he pulled her hard against him, planning to tell her by the strength of his hold just how much he cared.

Cared, yes.

But did he love her the way she deserved to be loved? At one point in their relationship, unequivocally, he'd loved her to that degree.

Once.

Nine years ago.

Did he still love her? He wished he knew.

He was attracted to her. But was that enough to base a lifelong marriage on? And as much as he owed it to his son to legitimately give him his last name, didn't he also owe it to him to promise to stand by him, as well as Allie, till death do them part? If Caleb was anything, he was loyal. He knew how to stick with something whether it be an assignment, family member or friend.

This marriage thing was different.

His *entire* life, spent with a woman who'd already destroyed him. If she pulled up and left town again, this time with their son, Caleb wouldn't survive it.

Her voice soft, scratchy and vulnerable, she said, "Your family, and anyone else you care to invite for Halloween is welcome in my home."

He raised his eyebrows. "Even Giselle?"

"STILL GONNA DO *Captain Underpants* for your book report?" Cal asked his best friend, Sam. He'd have rather asked at school instead of over the phone, but his stupid mom still wouldn't let him go.

"Nah," Sam said. "I have to switch to a bigger book 'cause Mom says there's too many pictures in that one."

"Sorry. That sucks."

Sam asked, "You still gonna do that alien book?"

"I want to," Cal said, spinning in his mom's big office desk chair. "But Mom says it's too scary."

"What's your dad say?"

"He's cool with it."

"Man," Sam said, "you gotta get them married so your dad'll be around all the time to make your mom be nice all the time."

"Really?" Cal asked.

"That's what Clara says. And Reider says Clara *likes you* likes you, so I *know* she wouldn't lie."

"Eeuuw!" Making a face that'd be worse than one he'd make while drinking maggot blood, Cal asked, "She *likes me* likes me?"

"Yep."

"Man." Cal thumped his forehead on the desk. "I've sure got a lot of problems."

"WHAT ARE YOU DOING?" Allie asked Caleb over lunch in her office. They'd ordered in Chinese from the restaurant at the end of the block. Cal was down the hall with his Uncle Adam and a couple of the other marshals, who weren't standing guard at either entrance to her chambers.

"What's it look like I'm doing?" he said, drizzling sweet and sour sauce over her pork.

"Thanks." Grinning, she shook her head. "How'd you know I needed more?"

"You always did when every molecule of your rice wasn't orange. Sorry, I was on autopilot, assuming you still do the same."

"I do," she said after taking another bite. "Funny, huh?"

"What?" he asked, watching her bite the corner off a soy sauce packet, then squirt it on his beef broccoli. Mmm… The naughty things she used to do with those pearly whites. "Oh—thank you."

"You're welcome." She took a napkin from the pile in the center of her work table to wipe brown liquid from her fingers. Darned shame—her wasting good sauce on a napkin when he could've licked it off! "Don't you think it's weird how we remember so much about each other? So many goofy things. When we're not fighting, it's like we've never been apart."

"What do you think it means?" he asked.

"Not sure," she said. "But if you'd ask my mom, she'd no doubt tell you it's a sign I never should've left you in the first place."

"How's she doing?" he asked, helping himself to a bite of her pork.

"Great. Always busy with some new hobby or her garden. Her latest passion is refinishing antiques."

He winced. "Sounds more like torture than fun."

"What? The Flea Market King wouldn't like fixing up old furniture?"

"Hey, I just buy the stuff. What happens to it from there is woman's work." He winked.

She landed a playful slug to his shoulder.

"Seriously, how about inviting your mom for Halloween, too?"

Allie froze. "You think?" It would be tough facing Caleb's family. Having her mom there beside her would be a comfort. Wouldn't it? Or would she for once give voice to the disapproval Allie knew she felt?

"Sure," Caleb said. "Why not? It'll be good for everyone to get to know each other."

"Okay, then, thanks," she said, warmed that he'd thought of including her mom in what would hopefully, after some understandable initial awkwardness, be a fun occasion.

"Wonder what my mom would have thought of our situation?" he asked.

Allie's pulse was suddenly racing, as she wasn't all that sure she wanted to know. "Your mom would probably be furious with me for keeping her grandson from her all these years."

"Not necessarily," he said. "I think she'd be mad at me for not going after you. Moving heaven and earth to bring you home." He swirled his food with his fork. "Mom was real big on family." With a wistful chuckle, he said, "I think she'd planned all of our weddings by the time we were five. Lots of themed stuff. Beau was supposed to have a Valentine's Day ceremony. I was St Patrick's Day. Gillian got Christmas and Adam the Fourth of July."

"Did Gillian follow through with your mom's plan?"

"Nah. But in reverence to her, she did put a sprig of mistletoe on a special place setting at her head table."

"Aw, how sweet," Allie said. "Hearing that makes me like Gillian more—and your mom. I'm sorry you lost her."

"Me, too," he said. "She was a great testament to the song, 'Only the Good Die Young.'"

The sadness in Caleb's eyes had Allie saying the first thing she could think of to get his mind on a more cheerful subject. "Aren't these walls the ugliest, most dingy color you've ever seen?"

He glanced around the room. "If you say so. Can't say as I've ever noticed."

She laughed. "That's a man for you."

"Hey, watch it. I'm a great decorator."

"Okay then," she said, setting down her fork. "What color would you paint this room?"

"I don't know," he said around another bite of her lunch. "White?"

Making a buzzer sound, she said. "Try again."

"Brown? Blue? Red?"

"No, no and no. Jungle-green might be nice. Or a rich, vibrant cobalt."

Making a face, he said, "What's tha—"

The office door burst open. "Caleb," Bear said. "We got trouble."

He was instantly on his feet. "Cal?"

"Right here." Bear shuttled the boy into the room.

Caleb kissed Allie's forehead, then the top of his son's head, then left the room, locking the door behind him.

"What's going on?" Cal asked, the sage green eyes that matched his father's, wide, questioning and worried.

"Don't know," Allie said, pulling him into a hug. "Guess we'll just have to sit tight till Caleb comes back to tell us."

If he comes back.

Oh god. She blinked back the sudden tears. She didn't want Caleb out there in the line of danger. He should be in here, safe with them.

Is this what it would be like being married to him? Living in a perpetual state of fear? If she felt this awful, what was Cal going through?

"You okay, baby?" she asked, stroking his fine dark hair.

"I'm not a baby," he said, wriggling away. "You got any more sweet and sour stuff? I'm still hungry."

"How can you be hungry at a time like this?"

"Like what?" He was already helping himself to the contents of her plate.

"Cal? What's the matter with you? Your dad is in danger at this very moment. Thank goodness everyone else went out for lunch. Who knows what could be happening out there? People shooting or rioting or who knows what."

"Mom, you need to chill. Caleb's a marshal. He's got a gun and stuff. He knows what to do if anyone shoots at him."

After a few loaded seconds of staring at her suddenly wise son with her mouth wide open, Allie pulled herself together. Wow. When had her son gotten so mature?

Allie had a long time to ponder her question as it was an hour before she heard a knock. She scrambled up from her uneasy perch on the sofa, running for her office door. "Caleb?"

"Sorry," Adam said. "Just me."

"Oh." Her shoulders sagged.

"Make a guy feel welcome," Adam said with a crooked grin. Was that a good sign? Surely he couldn't smile if—

"I'd make you feel welcome," she said. "If you'd just—"

"My dad okay?" Cal asked.

"Yeah." Adam patted the boy's head. "Just caught up in paperwork. He'll be at the house later."

"Cool," Cal said, bounding back to his Legos. "Told you so, Mom."

"Told you what?" Adam asked.

"Just that I shouldn't be worried about Caleb." Allie hugged herself. She was suddenly freezing, and more than a little shaky with relief. "That he knows what he's doing. He's good at his job."

Adam laughed. "You needed a kid to tell you that?"

Allie made a face at him before grilling the brother of the man to whom she was growing dangerously attached for details on exactly why Cal and her had been locked in her office for a big chunk of the afternoon.

"'Bout time you got here," Allie said to Caleb as he strolled into the living room. It was nine-thirty. The meat loaf dinner she'd prepared for him had long since dried out, and their son had gone to bed.

"Miss me?" he asked, leaning against the fireplace wall, looking more handsome than any man had a right to. His smile tightened her insides. Dried her mouth. Had just the sight of him always had this effect?

"Maybe." She wished she felt as calm as she sounded.

He laughed. "Guess that's better than not at all."

Not in the mood for games, she put the brief she'd been reading on the floor, then went to him, curving her arms around him. "All right, yes," she said against his chest, breathing in his smell, only enhanced by the latest rain and the sweet, smoky scent of a neighbor's wood-burning fireplace. "I missed you. I worried about you. I've been utterly and completely out of my mind.

There—" She pulled away and grinned up at him. "Happy?"

"Yeah." He wrapped her in a blanket of a hug.

"Hungry?" she asked.

She felt him shake his head. "Just tired."

"I'll bet. Adam told me what happened."

Pulling away, he took her hand, drawing her toward the sofa. When they'd gotten comfortable, he said, "Ballsy of our friend Francis to think he could pull it off—blowing up the whole courthouse. This time, though, he screwed up big-time. We got at least twenty of his pals." He winced. "Of course this means more work for you in helping to prosecute all of them, but—"

"If it means once and for all cleaning up our corner of the world," Allie said, thinking of the cultlike compound Francis had established that housed so many families who stood against every principle America had been founded upon. Calling themselves the Disciples of Truth, local authorities had long known of Francis's organization but had been shocked to discover just how large it was. "I'm ready."

"Good."

"So?" She drew her legs up beside her, angling to face him. "Now that you've made a huge dent in Francis's posse, when are you heading back?"

"To Portland?"

She nodded, hating the lump in her throat that'd formed the second she'd even thought the question, let alone asked it. Though the trial wasn't over yet, surely the Disciples had been crippled to the point that they could no longer function. "You are going back, aren't you? I mean now that Cal and I are no longer in danger…."

A myriad of emotions flashed over his face. "So that's it, then? Now that I caught the bad guys, you want me gone?"

"No," she said. "I was just asking. You know, wondering if this meant your boss would call you back to the Portland office."

"Sorry," he said, "but you're not officially getting rid of me until after Francis is sentenced. That said, it should be all right for Cal to go back to school once the jury reaches a verdict."

"Good." She licked her lips, looking to the fire instead of the suddenly unreadable mask Caleb had made of his features.

"We still on for Halloween if you wrap up by then? Reason I ask is that my sister called my cell about an hour ago. She's coordinating travel plans and a party. Guess she's even booked a few rooms at a local B and B. The Morning Glory Inn. Heard of it?"

"Sure. It's a beautiful place. The owner's a friend. Now, can we please get back to discussing the important stuff?"

He pushed himself up, stood in front of the fire. "Didn't know we were discussing anything important."

"That's not fair."

He shook his head. Laughed. "Mind telling me what is?"

Hands to her forehead, she said, "This afternoon, when Cal and I were holed up in my office, not knowing what was going on, I couldn't believe the things going through my head. One minute I was cursing you, blaming you for my son and I somehow ending up in this mess…"

"And the next?"

She clenched her jaw.

She'd cursed herself. For not marrying Caleb *now*. Most of all, for not marrying him then. Because at least then she would've had nine idyllic years with him. Cal would've have known his father. She would've stored a lifetime of memories to keep her warm for dozens of years to come.

She shook her head. "I'm sorry."

"You should be," he said with a sharp laugh. "I'm so sick and tired of you blaming me for every little thing that goes wrong in your life, Al. I'm a man. Not some danger magnet."

"I know," she said, bowing her head.

"Do you know, Allie? Do you have any idea of the life we could share?" He crossed back to her, knelt before her, eased his hand under her chin, smoothing his fingers along her throat, the pad of his thumb over her lips.

Yes, she almost said, but since she couldn't form the word, she simply nodded. "I was so afraid of losing you today."

"But you didn't."

"I didn't."

"But now that the crisis has passed, you're right back where you started, wondering what you're going to do with me?"

Since she didn't know what to say to him, she settled for throwing her arms around his neck, crushing him in a hug. "Make love to me," she said. "Please."

He groaned.

"*Please,* Caleb."

Drawing back, he asked, "Why?"

"Does it matter?"

He looked away, then back. "Yeah, we could sleep together, but what then? I'm here to protect you. That's my job. Ethically, sleeping with you would go against every professional oath I've taken. And what happens in the morning? When I want to make you my wife, and Cal my son in every sense of the word, and you run away again?"

"That's not fair," Allie railed. "Just because I'm not going to marry you, doesn't mean I'm running. I already told you I would *never* do that again. I was wrong the first time. Why would I do it a second? How could I? There's my job. Cal's school. The logistics alone—it would never work."

"That mean you've considered it?"

"That hurts, Caleb. Really hurts."

"I know," he said, mouth set hard. "Better than anyone—I know. Oh, and I picked up a real palm tree for your bedroom. It's in the kitchen. Thought your cold-ass sleeping quarters needed some life. 'Course that was before you gave me an invitation to join you."

Chapter Eight

"You nervous?" Caleb asked two days later upon entering the courtroom. The jury had just given word that they'd reached a verdict. It'd taken less than thirty minutes for the sentence to come down.

"About what?"

"How fast all of this happened. The trial. The verdict."

She flashed him a weak smile. "Guess I'm trying not to think about it. Thanks for reminding me."

"My pleasure. Oh, and for the record, we haven't had much chance to talk lately, and so anyway, sorry about what I said about your bedroom. It's actually kind of hot in there—or at least could be." He thrilled her with a quick, ultrahunky wink before slipping into Rambo mode, checking to make sure the coast was clear and talking into the microphone hidden up his sleeve. As much as Allie hated what Caleb did for a living, even she had to admit, he did look kind of—all right, *a lot*—sexy when he was doing his marshal thing.

When on duty, he became a chameleon, adjusting his clothes to blend with the scenery. In deference to their current courtroom setting, he wore a black suit, rumpled white shirt and navy tie. In college, she used to starch his shirts before their mock court sessions, lovingly smoothing her fingertips along the crisp cotton. She'd also helped him with the knots on his ties, because she'd loved easing her fingers inside his shirt collar, feeling the warm, smooth skin of his neck.

"All's clear," he said, jolting her out of an entirely inappropriate daydream.

Hoping the hot rush of awareness seizing her system was only evident to her, she gruffly thanked him, then proceeded to her bench.

One look at the victims' exhausted families was all it took to bring reality back. Those poor, devastated people. No one should lose loved ones before they'd lived a long, happy life. And to lose them in such a brutal, senseless manner....

Allie gritted her teeth.

Innocent until proven guilty.

The bailiff led in the jury. The two oldest women looked as if they may have been crying.

A good sign or bad?

Save for a far-off sniffle on the back row, the jury was painfully quiet.

Allie looked to the jury forewoman. Eve Parks. A pretty brunette, single mom to three doe-eyed little girls. She was also an accountant. Owned Uncle Sam's Tax Service on the corner of Elm and Provincial. The defense fought hard to have her disqualified. In front of the converted gas station she used as an office stood a twelve-foot statue of Uncle Sam. She and the girls changed his clothes and hat to match the different holiday seasons. To the defense's way of thinking, this automatically made her an overly patriotic postal-worker lover, and therefore, biased.

To Allie's way of thinking, it made her American.

No more biased than any other hardworking, law-abiding citizen in the courtroom who had an innate disgust for their fellow, hardworking citizens being blown to bits while standing in line to mail a package to Cousin Ima in Duluth.

Allie took a deep breath, then asked, "Has the jury reached a verdict?"

"We have your honor. We the jury find the defendant, Francis William Ashford, guilty on all counts."

Pandemonium broke out.

On those siding with the victims, jubilant cries.

On those praying for the defense, bone-chilling sobs.

"Commie bitch is what you are!" Francis shouted at Allie while bailiffs led him from the room. "You're gonna die! I don't give a damn if they wanna fry me, you're gonna die before I go!"

She'd barely had time to process the man's words before Caleb and Bear whisked her away to the shocking calm of the hall leading to her chambers.

"You all right?" Caleb asked.

Though she wasn't quite sure, she managed a nod. "The sentencing. I need to go back in. A date has to be set."

"It'll wait. Let's get that mob quieted down. Bear," Caleb said, "take Al on to her office. Make sure she gets a snack."

The giant of a marshal eyed him funny. "A snack?" he said out of Allie's earshot.

Caleb sighed. "Cut me some slack, okay? She refused to eat breakfast. I know how she gets when she doesn't eat. Hell, we might end up having to protect Francis from her."

"You being careful?" Bear asked.

"Come again?"

Bear checked out Allie's office, ushered her in, then shut the door before continuing. "We all like you, Caleb—a lot. Which is why no one's said anything about you guarding your own son, and for all practical purposes your wife."

"Whoa," Caleb said. "For the record, Allie's not my wife. Nothing's happened that shouldn't have." Except for a few damned hot kisses that he'd wanted to take a lot further.

"Hey," Bear said, massive paw of a hand on his shoulder, "it's all cool. You don't have to defend your actions to me. I just know you have a lot higher ambitions than the rest of us schmucks. I wouldn't want anything tarnishing your shiny silver star. You know, mucking up your stab at turning it gold."

"Think I should take myself off the case?" Caleb looked away. Sighed. "I gotta admit, even for myself, there's a couple times the line has been blurred."

Bear shrugged. "You're the only one who can make that call."

THREE WEEKS HAD PASSED since the end of Francis's trial. Due to defense appeals, the sentencing phase— typically eleven weeks after a ruling—could be months away. Fortunately, Francis seemed to have accepted his

fate, as had those in his posse who weren't already behind bars. Which was why Allie had insisted upon loos-
ening up both her own and Cal's security. Not that they
wouldn't still have round-the-clock protection, just that
in her, and Caleb's, professional judgment, Cal could
safely return to school as long as he was accompanied
by a security detail. Allie also hoped a few well-planned
weekend outings would ease his feelings of frustration
and isolation, as well as her own lingering pangs of im-
pending doom.

"This is so good for him—for both of us," Allie said
Saturday afternoon at a petting farm ten miles outside
of town. The place was straight out of a storybook,
complete with a big, red barn and rambling white farm-
house where they'd eaten lunch. The day itself, an
Oregon jewel. Perfect sun. Perfect temperature. Perfectly blue sky capping the perfect day.

Cal sat in a small, grassy enclosure, giggling under
the weight of two licking baby goats.

"It's good for me, too," Caleb said. "Despite having
to drag them around." He eyed his brother.

Adam waved.

Allie waved back. "I know now that things have calmed
down around here, you all are probably bored, but thanks
for sticking by us. The end of Francis's trial was dicey, and
it's a comfort knowing you'll be around for the long haul."

"Sure," he said, awkwardly looking off toward a
chicken coop, like he wasn't sure what to do with her
appreciation.

She held her hand out to a pony, letting him nuzzle
her open palm.

"Try this." Caleb put a quarter in a feed machine, then gave her the grains.

She did and the pony went wild, snorting and licking her palm. His hot breath and fuzzy lips tickled and for the first time in days, she laughed.

"Euw," she said, wiping her slobbered hand on Caleb's denim shirt. It was missing a button near the collar and at that moment, old and new affection for him made her want to mend his shirt along with their relationship.

"Hey!" he complained. "Wipe your pony spit on your own clothes."

"Oh," she teased, "but it looks so much better on yours."

"Come here," he said, leading her by both her hands to a hand-pump. Freeing one of her hands, he worked the pump, getting her good and wet, then, pressing soap from the dispenser, slowly rubbing her palms and fingers with cool, slick suds. His service felt more like a massage than hand-washing, but she wasn't complaining. To the contrary, she closed her eyes and smiled. "Ahh, this is the life."

"Yeah," he said. "If you're the one getting pampered."

She opened her eyes to catch his smile.

"So?" he asked. "What's your verdict on the rooster?"

"The city really said it's okay?"

"Yep. Your house is just outside city limits. You've got enough land out back that you could even have a cow, horse and that donkey Cal's been wanting."

"Gee, great. Like I don't have enough on my plate already?"

"The kid needs a pet, Al."

"We'll get him a goldfish. He can have some of that fancy colored decorator gravel. But a rooster? Where are we going to put him? What are the neighbors going to say when he starts crowing Sunday morning?"

"Who cares about the neighbors? As for a shelter," Caleb said, "I was thinking me and Cal could build something. For now, for Cal's safety, we'd do the actual construction in the garage, but it shouldn't be too hard to then move the coop out to the yard."

"Why are you pushing so hard for this?" Allie asked.

"I don't know." Caleb plucked a late-blooming daisy from alongside the gravel trail and tucked it behind her left ear. "Just thought it might be fun. You know, a father-son project."

Allie knew she should say ixnay on the backyard barnyard, but one added benefit besides Cal and his dad doing something fun together, was that even after Caleb returned to Portland, Cal would still have the pet to remember him by. "Okay," she said. "You twisted my arm. But you two farmers have to build the coop before you get chickens."

"Agreed."

"How long you think it'll take?" she asked.

"Maybe a week. Two tops."

Shading her eyes from the sun, she asked, "That's not long, considering there's still six weeks after that till Francis learns his ultimate fate and you head back to Portland."

"Nope," he said, his tone unreadable. "Six weeks. Not long at all."

She trailed her hand along the smooth corral rail. "What then, Caleb? What happens to us after the trial?"

"Simple. We figure out a shared custody agreement, or…" The obvious hung between them. If she didn't willingly give Caleb a large portion of their son's time, he'd take her to court. "Work with me, Allie. There's no reason for any of this to go beyond your kitchen table. We'll just sit down with a calendar and figure out how we want to divvy Cal's time."

Her throat tightened. Still, she nodded. The last thing she wanted was to see Cal dragged into court. Lord knew, she spent enough time on the bench. She sure didn't want to be on the other side, too.

"I know this must be rough on you," Caleb said, his large hand strong and warm on her back. "Thanks for being civilized abut it."

"Sure. I want what's best for our son."

"Me, too, Allie." He paused where they'd been walking alongside the corral. "So what are we talking? I'll take school vacations? A big chunk of his summer?"

"Then when I do I get to see him?" Allie asked.

"Every night after school," Caleb said. "Every weekend. I mean, I'll for sure drive down whenever I can, but—"

"No. I understand." Allie started walking. Fast. As fast as she possibly could.

"Then why are you running from me?"

"I'm not running."

He snatched her by her shoulders, spinning her around. "Then talk to me. It doesn't have to be this way. Neither of us should be sad. I mean, while I've got Cal, take a vacation. A pottery class. Try having a social life."

She closed her eyes. Swallowed hard.

Allie didn't want a social life.

She wanted her son.

Truth be told, what she really wanted was a family, the way it might've been with Caleb. If only he loved her enough to give up his death wish of a career. If only he wanted the same things she did. A nice home. Lazy evening dinners and Saturdays spent in the garden or riding go-carts at the park. But Caleb wanted none of that. She knew, because he could have had all that and more nine years ago when she'd first told him she was pregnant.

"Are you even listening to me?" he asked, holding her captive in his beautiful, sage green stare. "You don't have a choice, Allie. You have to at least be willing to give shared custody a chance. I'm not going away."

"Oh, for crying out loud," Adam said, pausing to pet a pony while strolling their way. "Why don't you two just shut up already? Did you forget you're wired for sound?"

Allie shook her head. Bloody fantastic. As if the constant bickering wasn't bad enough, she'd forgotten they had an audience.

"If you don't mind me saying so," Adam said, taking a smashed Snickers from his jeans pocket. The pony sauntered up, apparently to check out the new smell. "Me and the guys took a vote, and bro, seems to us this whole matter could be solved easily enough by you just telling her how it's going to be."

"Oh, really?" Allie said, hands on her hips. "And tell me, Adam, how are things *going to be*—according to the guys?"

"First," Adam said around a big bite of candy bar, "my brother's got to propose. Then, you've got to accept. Then, the way we see it, the two of you—and Cal—live happily ever after."

Caleb snorted. "Great plan, there, stud. Only one problem."

"What's that?" Adam asked, cramming the last half of the candy into his mouth.

"I have no intention of proposing."

"That's good," Allie said. "Because I have no intention of accepting."

"HE'S *REALLY* YOUR DAD?" Billy Stubbs asked Cal in gym class Monday morning.

"Yep." Cal couldn't help but puff out his chest with pride.

"And you really didn't know?" his friend Nathan asked.

"Nope. Mom lied. She said he was dead."

His friend Reider whistled. He was the only one in their class who could do it, so when he did, everyone paid lots of attention. "You mad at your mom?"

"Yeah. Wouldn't you be?"

Clara Holmes, whose parents had been divorced twice, making her an expert, said, "I've been thinking, you should use this to get a new Xbox. Maybe even an electric scooter."

"Really?" Cal's eyes got all big.

"You should listen to her, Cal," Bart Henning said.

"I know my parents only got divorced once, but you can get lots of good stuff. All you gotta do is act all sad—but not so sad they make you go to a head doctor. Just sad enough that they buy you lots of good stuff to cheer you up. Right before Dad moved out, I got a new baseball bat and glove and gobs of candy."

"Cool!" Billy said. "I wish my mom and dad would break up."

"You gonna live with your dad now?" Clara asked.

"I don't know," Cal said. "I s'pose."

Clara said, "You know that means you *never* get to see your mom again?"

"Really?" Cal looked around at his group of friends, and every one of them was nodding.

Except for Billy—he was picking his nose.

"When my mom got her second divorce," Clara said, "we had to move here. I never get to see my real dad anymore. So if your parents get divorced, you're gonna have to pick."

"But I don't even think they're married," Cal said.

"They *have* to be married," Billy said. "Elsewise how'd they have you?"

"Oh, yeah." Cal sighed. "So if I go with Dad, does that mean I don't get to keep my room and bike and stuff? Or do I get to just kick Mom out and tell Dad to stay?"

"You'd kick your mom out?" Sam asked. "She makes good cupcakes."

"I know," Cal said. "But she lied."

"Yeah," Sam said. "Guess she'll have to go."

Clara said, "One thing you better do before you get

rid of your mom is find out if your dad knows how to cook. Otherwise you'll have to eat pizza every night."

"What's wrong with that?" Billy asked.

"Sounds good at first," Clara said, "but trust me. After eating nothing but pizza every night for years and years and years, you get sick of it."

"HEY, BABY," Allie said when she walked in the back door late that afternoon, finding Cal at the table doing homework. "Look what I brought for dinner. Your favorite." Careful not to drop it, she waved the pizza box she'd had to beg her driver to take her to pick up.

He gave her a funny look, then went right back to long division.

"How'd you do in gym today? Make anymore soccer touchdowns?"

He shook his head. "And they're called *goals*. Touchdowns are for football."

"Cal…" She took a deep breath. "Are we ever going to be friends again, or are you going to keep being mad?"

"Being mad."

"Okay…" She set the pizza box on the counter and slipped off her coat, tossing it over the back of the chair. "Baby, I know you still have times when you're angry with me about your dad, so if you want to yell at me, go for it."

He said nothing, just sat there, staring at his paper.

"I get it that you're ticked I lied," Allie said. "I'm sorry. *Really* sorry. But at the time, it seemed like the best thing to do."

"And now?" he said. "Would you do it again?"

What a big question from a little boy. "Truthfully," she said, easing onto the seat beside him, "I'm not sure."

"You always tell me never to lie to you. How come you're allowed to lie to me?"

Allie swallowed hard. "You're right," she said. "It wasn't very nice of me—or fair—to lie to you. But at the time, I didn't know what else to do."

"That's stupid," he said with a vehemence she hadn't known he possessed. "You taught me honesty's the best policy. But that's only for kids?"

"No, honey." She sighed. Swiped her fingers through her hair. "When I lied, I thought I was protecting you."

"From Dad? Is he dangerous?"

"No. Of course not. Caleb—he's a wonderful man. Kind, considerate. Brave. He's one of the best men I've ever known."

"Then how come you didn't want him to be my dad?"

"Good question." *Very* good question.

"HE ASLEEP?" Allie asked Caleb later that night. While he'd tucked in their son, she'd been in the living room, reading the same page of her latest stack of court briefs for the fifteenth time.

"Yeah," he said.

"Did he want to talk about it?"

By *it*, they both knew what she meant. He'd been in a mood all afternoon. Caleb shook his head. "All he wanted to know was when I'm getting his rooster. Guess some girl at school told him since we're getting a divorce, he gets presents."

Allie wrinkled her nose. "But we're not even married."

"Try telling that to Clara. Seems she knows more about life than either of us."

"Clara." Allie sighed. "That's another kid I've never heard of. Where are they coming from?"

Caleb shrugged, helping himself to the lounge chair beside her. "You ever miss having a wood-burning fire?" he asked, staring into the sterile gas flames.

"Sometimes. I miss the smell mostly. Remember that cabin we rented our sophomore year? It had a gorgeous rock fireplace. I ate so many s'mores I thought I'd barf."

"Tell me about it," he said. "And here I'd forked out big bucks to spend a wild night in the bedroom—not to watch you hug the bathroom throne."

"Sorry," she said with a misty smile. They'd been so good together back then. Right up until she'd gotten pregnant, she'd never considered spending the rest of her life with anyone but him. He'd been everything to her. And maybe some small part of her had secretly hoped his love for her would be enough to sway him into practicing office law instead of the Wild West variety.

When she'd told him she was pregnant, she'd secretly expected him to fall to his knees, proposing that not only they immediately merge their private lives into a marriage, but their professional lives into a shared private practice. When after a week of his knowing about the baby, he hadn't done either of those things, she'd gone into defense mode. Saving not only her spirit, but her pride. The "losing the baby" story—sheer desperation. For if she couldn't have all of Caleb—his absolute love and support of their marriage along with his commitment to keep himself safe for not just her, but their baby—she didn't want him at all. *Couldn't* want him. For the day-to-day terror of not knowing if he'd walk through her front door—or a pair of fellow marshals, to tell her of his untimely death—would not only be the death of their marriage, but her.

"What're you thinking about?" he asked, still staring into the flames.

"Life," she said. "How differently things turned out from what I'd expected."

"You mean us?"

She nodded.

"That night," he said. "At your rental house? The last night we fought. I left…"

"Yes?" She leaned closer.

"A few days later, I came back. I wanted you to marry me. But you were gone."

She closed her eyes for a moment, willing her pulse to slow. "Were you also planning on ditching your plans to become a marshal?"

"No. And since when was my entering the marshal's service even an issue?"

"Since the day you first told me that's what you wanted to do."

"That's b.s., Al."

"Oh, so just because your personal safety is a hang-up of mine, it's b.s.? Remember, Caleb, it was you who left that night—not me."

"Yeah, but you'd just handed me this bomb. What was I supposed to do?"

Her eyes welled.

"Don't you get weepy," he said. "Not when you were the one who ultimately ran away. I came back for you. I was going to marry you. Make it right. But no-o-o, you'd taken the coward's way out by running off. Oh, that was real mature."

She shook her head. "See? Even in the midst of this beautiful speech about how you'd come back for me to ask me to marry you, you still throw out that wretched phrase."

"What phrase?" he demanded.

"Making it right," she said with a cocky sway of her head. *"Ooooh,* now that's every girl's dream proposal. That's right on up there on the romance scale. Ties with winning a bride in a poker tourney."

"Look," he said. "Just because—"

Caleb's cell rang.

"Dammit," he said under his breath. "Sorry. Better get it." He flicked open the phone, the whole while never breaking her stare. "This is Caleb."

"Hey there, son. I hear congratulations are in order."

"Dad. Um, hang on a sec."

"Sure," his father said.

He covered the mouthpiece, then stood, saying to Allie, "Be right back. And I want to pick up right where we left off."

"Me, too," she said, eyes suspiciously misty.

Caleb walked to the kitchen. "Okay," he said. "Now I can talk."

"You on duty?" his dad asked.

"No."

"Then why couldn't you talk before?"

"Geez, Dad. Does it matter?"

"You weren't trying to steal another kiss from your boy's momma, were you?"

Caleb groaned. He could just see the grin lighting his old man's eyes.

"Good grief," Caleb said. "My sister has the biggest mouth this side of the Mississippi. And no—I wasn't trying to kiss Allie. Just talk."

"I liked her," his dad said. "Seemed like she had a good head on her shoulders. Well, at least until... But since she didn't lose the baby after all, well... Why didn't you ask her to marry you the second you found out she was pregnant? That would've been the honorable thing to do. I raised you better than—"

"I was going to ask her to marry me. She took off."

"Oh."

"Yeah, oh. So I don't see why my family is all of a sudden taking her side."

"There are no sides here, son, except for your boy's. We just want to welcome him into our family. Making nice with his mom is a big first step."

"I know," Caleb said. "So can I please get back to doing just that?"

After enduring a brief lecture on never being too old to be scolded for talking back to his father, Caleb finally hung up and headed back to the living room.

Where Allie had fallen asleep.

He was covering her with the red blanket from the back of the sofa when she bolted awake. "Sorry," he said. "Didn't mean to startle you."

"That's okay." She covered her mouth while yawning.

"Sorry about the call," he said. "Guess I should've let voice mail answer."

"It was your father," she said. "You had to get it. And quit apologizing for everything, Caleb. You didn't do anything wrong."

"Then how come I feel like I've done nothing but screw up ever since I got here? Especially when you're the one who had a secret."

"Ouch."

"Am I wrong?" He raised his eyebrows.

"No," she said. "But I'm tired. Tired of fighting. Of worrying about Cal's safety and my own…."

He sat in the chair beside her and she curled onto her side, looking sleepy and beautiful and vulnerable.

"Just for the rest of this night, Caleb, can't we call a truce?"

"Sure," he said, against his better judgment. He was ready to grant her anything, anytime.

Chapter Nine

Not long after their truce, talk drifted to making up for lost time—namely, swapping dating disasters. "Didn't you forget one?" Allie asked.

Grimacing, Caleb said, "Once you've had a blind date with a female mortician who's idea of a good time is finding just the right hairstyle for her latest *client*…" His wince pretty much finished his sentence.

Sipping her mint tea, trying to pretend her next question didn't mean as much as it did, she asked, "What about the woman from the I-5 Waffle Hut?"

He sat up straighter. "Where'd you hear about her?"

Allie's stomach fell. He wasn't trying to hide the fact that he still had feelings for her, was he? "I, um, was talking with Adam one day and he brought her up."

"Mmm…Delores," he said with a wistful nod. "Along with a certain pair of large, melon-shaped assets, she made damn good coffee. Guess that's why I didn't mention her. She was more delicious than disaster."

Allie rolled her brief and swatted him.

"Ouch!" he complained. "What was that for?"

"I don't know. Just felt like you needed it."

"Why?" he teased with a cocky grin that stirred heat all the way to her toes. "You threw me away. Shouldn't the rest of the world's female population have a shot?"

Allie was in trouble.

When Caleb was charming like this, he was at his most dangerous. He reminded her how much fun they used to have. How much life they used to share. But that was a long time ago. They were different people now.

"Okay, wait a minute," Caleb said. "I told you about Delores and Penny, who played beauty shop on dead people. When do I get the scoop on your illustrious social life?"

"Ha!" Allie laughed. "What social life?"

"You can't be serious," Caleb said. "You're a hottie. How can I be your only guy?"

"Oh, puh-lease. I'd hardly call myself *hot*. And I didn't say you were my *only* guy. Just that I haven't dated that much."

"All right…." Leaning forward, rubbing his palms together, he said, "Let's hear it. Who was your last major fling?"

"Well…" It took her an embarrassing few seconds to even remember. Truthfully, usually after one or two dates, she knew she hadn't liked the guy even a fraction as much as the father of her son, so what had been the point in leading the guy on? "There was that hunky Juvie Court judge I had a wild fling with at the National Judicial Conference in Vegas."

"For real?" His eyebrows shot up.

"What's the matter, Cowboy Cal? You jealous?"

Caleb froze.

Cowboy Cal.

She used to call him that in the heat of sex. Based on his love of all things Wild West, it'd been their little joke. And judging by her flushed cheeks, he wasn't the only one who'd noticed her slip.

He cleared his throat. "Guess I should get back outside, huh? Let you get back to work."

"You on duty?" she asked.

"Nope. Officially off."

"Then stay," Allie couldn't believe what she'd just suggested. "I have a perfectly proper guest room. You can be here in the morning when Cal wakes up."

"I don't know," he said. "Doesn't sound kosher."

"You're probably right." She pretended to be busy tidying her court documents. "I don't even know why I asked."

"So? Why did you?" Caleb angled on his chair to better face her. She looked weary. Big, brown eyes tired and red. Long, blond strands had escaped her ponytail, lending her the look of a naughty little girl. When she was made up, Allie was a stunning woman. But he'd always liked her best like this. Natural. Honest. Or at least she used to be honest. Now, he wasn't sure what she was. Other than no longer his.

"Who knows why I asked." She sighed. "Maybe because once I tuck Cal in for the night, I get lonely."

Caleb knew that cost her a lot to admit.

"Then why not date?" he couldn't help but wonder out loud. "We've already established that you're hot."

"You established," she said with grin.

He rolled his eyes. "Bottom line, I'd think lots of guys would want to go out with you."

Casting him a wistful smile, she said, "That's just it. I've had guys want to go out with me, but I can't say I wanted to spend extended periods of time with any of them."

What about me? Did the fact that she wanted him there all night, sleeping just down the hall, bear any special significance?

"Sure. I get it," he said. And he truly did. Because he felt the same about not dating other women. Even when he found someone whose company he thought he could enjoy, once he got to know her, he'd discover her to be nothing like Allie. She wouldn't have her humor. Her drive and fire. Her goofy love of Chia Pets. But where did that leave them? Essentially, just because Allie and him had forged a tentative new friendship, it didn't mean anything. Not of significance. Their son was still at the heart of the trouble between them.

"Does that mean you'll stay?" she asked.

Flashing lights and sirens screamed *no!*

One look at those big brown eyes of hers and he couldn't say anything but, "Sure, um, just let me give a heads-up to my guys."

"HAVE EVERYTHING you need?" Allie asked, self-conscious in her ragtag flannel pj's and terry cloth robe. She stood on the threshold to the guest room—for tonight at least, Caleb's room. When her mother came down for the occasional visit, it'd never seemed cramped. But then, Allie's mom was only five foot two.

Allie licked her lips, trying with everything in her not to look at Caleb's powerful chest.

"Thanks for the offer," Caleb said. "But looks like I'm all set." He balled up his dirty shirt, flung it in the corner. "Nice place you've got here. Beats the hell out of my motel."

"Thanks," she said, unexpectedly touched that he approved of her home. The home she'd made for herself and his son. The home she'd secretly wished a thousand times over that Caleb loved her enough to share in every conceivable way.

"You're welcome."

"Got towels?" she asked.

"Yeah," he said, pointing to the leaning pile of them she'd planted on the end of his bed. "There's enough there for like two weeks."

"Right. I forgot. How about pillows? Blankets? Soap or shampoo? Razor? Well—all I have are girly ones, but—"

He looked deep into her eyes. Put his hand on her shoulder. The hand that led up his muscular bare forearm and bicep and shoulder she used to sink her teeth into when they made love. His chest was broader than it had been nine years ago. His scent an all-too-familiar, all-too-seductive blend of a long day mixed with evergreens and rain.

"Allie," he finally said. "I'm good. What are you really asking?"

She shook her head. "I'm not sure what you mean."

"You seem like you're stalling. There some reason why you don't want to go to bed?"

"No," she said with a firm shake of her head. "No reason at all. Just making sure you're comfortable."

"Very," he said. "You'd make a great innkeeper."

"Okay, then. Guess I'll see you in the morning."

Caleb flashed her a smile.

The one she returned didn't come close to reaching her eyes.

"I DON'T KNOW, CLARA," Cal said at recess the next morning. His dad stood a little ways away, talking with one of his other guards. "I did what you said, and thought about which parent I want to live with all last night. But I never did get to see if Dad knows how to cook, and Mom brought home pizza for dinner. What does that mean?"

"Sorry, but that's not a good sign." Clara made her eyes all big, then grabbed the end of one of her braids and started sucking on it.

"Well, I already know Mom's a good cook," Cal said. "And when I tried getting Dad to buy me a present, he said he would, but I still don't have it."

"What'd you ask for?" Sam asked.

"A donkey or a rooster."

All the kids who had gathered around the big shade tree next to the little slide laughed so hard they snorted.

"What's so funny?" Cal asked. "I've always wanted both those things."

"Dummy," Clara said. "You're supposed to ask for new Game Boy games and DVDs, *not* a donkey!"

"Well, I didn't know."

Hands on her hips, she said, "Well, now you do.

Your homework for tonight is to find out if your dad cooks. If he cooks *and* gets you a donkey, then go with him. Otherwise, you might want to stay with your mom."

Cal wrinkled his nose from confusion, but Clara was the expert, so he guessed he had to do whatever she said—even if it sounded lame. Otherwise he might not even get a rooster, let alone a donkey!

"Clara," he said once most of his guy friends had headed for the tire swings. "You sure you're right about all this? What if I don't want to choose? Is there any way I can have both Mom and Dad?"

Clara took a long time to think about that, then said, "I guess you could make sure they stay married."

"DAD?" CAL ASKED on the way home from school.

"Yeah?"

"I was curious. You ever cook?" The two of them sat in the backseat of a cool, black SUV with really dark tinted windows. That big guy, Bear, drove.

"Sure," his dad said. "All the time."

"Like what kinds of stuff?"

"I don't know. Guy stuff. SpaghettiOs. TV dinners. Mac and cheese."

"Yeah, but do you ever make *Mom* stuff? You know, like birthday cake and pancakes and Great-Grandma Beatrice's meat loaf and spaghetti?"

"I make good oatmeal."

"That's it?" Cal pressed.

"What are you trying to get at?" his dad asked.

"Sounds to me," Bear said, "like he's feeling you out."

"For what?" Caleb asked.

Cal laughed when his dad gave him a noogie. Even if his dad couldn't cook, he was awfully fun to play with. When he stopped laughing long enough to breath, he said, "I'm askin' you questions 'cause this girl Clara says I gotta know if you can do certain stuff."

"How come?" His dad had a funny look on his face.

"'Cause she said now that you and Mom are getting divorced, I gotta pick which one to live with. She said whatever I do, I don't want to pick the one who can't cook, or else we won't have anything to eat but pizza. I like it a lot, and Clara says if you eat it every night, then you won't like it anymore."

"Hmm," his dad said. "This Clara sounds like a pretty smart girl—except for the part about me and your mom getting a divorce. That'd be kind of hard considering we're not married."

"But Billy said you couldn't have had me if you never got married."

Bear and Caleb laughed at that.

"Why's that funny?" Cal asked.

"Wait a few years, kid." Bear pulled the SUV into Cal's driveway.

"Bear?" his dad asked. "Mind giving me and Cal a few minutes?"

Bear gave his dad an army kind of salute-thing, then jumped out of the car.

"What'd you wanna talk to me about?" Cal asked. "When we're gonna get my donkey and rooster?"

"Sorry," his dad said. "But it might be a while." He

looked out the window for a minute, then back to him. "Cal, I'm noticing a trend I'm not comfortable with."

"What's a trend?" Cal asked.

Caleb touched his forehead, not sure where to begin. Where's a dictionary when you need one? "A trend is something that happens over and over. Like the way you keep bringing up this Clara girl and her ideas on what you should be saying and doing."

"Yeah," Cal said. "But she's been divorced twice, so she knows everything about it."

"I'm sure she does," Caleb said, patting his kid's knee. "And I'm not saying she doesn't know a lot. But in this case—in *our* family's case—maybe she doesn't know quite as much as she should."

"That what we are, Dad? A family? Me, you and Mom?"

Caleb cleared his throat. "That's what I'd like to be."

"Then will you and Mom be married? And live together and kiss and stuff?"

Groaning, Caleb was almost afraid to ask... "Where'd you hear that?"

"Sam. He says when you get married, you hafta kiss. I'm not ever gettin' married, but I guess if you want to marry my mom, even though she lied to you, that'd be okay."

"Thanks for the permission," Caleb said. "But I really can't see me and your mom tying the knot anytime soon."

"What's knot tying mean?"

"Just a fancy way for saying you're married."

Cal scrunched his nose. "So then you don't want to marry Mom?"

"Dude, give me a break." Caleb sighed. "Getting married isn't all that easy."

"Sure, it is. All you hafta do is rent a tux and Mom has to buy a white dress. Clara said."

"Oh, well," Caleb laughed. "If Clara said it's that easy, must be."

"So then you're gonna marry Mom?"

"YOU DIDN'T HAVE TO COOK," Allie said that night in the kitchen. "We could've ordered take-out. And I'm crazy about the canisters. You didn't have to bring those, either, but…" She grinned. "I'm glad you did. Thanks."

"You're welcome," Caleb said, matching her smile.

The giant tomato, eggplant and carrot canisters looked great in the kitchen. Allie adored the bright colors. Almost as much as she loved the fact that Caleb had been the one to give them to her. And speaking of items she loved, Mr. Chia Head had finally sprouted hair!

Cal was upstairs doing homework.

She sat on a bar stool, dressed in her comfy flannel pj's and white robe. "If you don't mind me asking, what brought on this domestic streak?"

He snorted. "Remember Clara?"

"Unfortunately, yes. What's she up to?"

"Seems she's been coaching Cal on how to best *handle* us," he said with a grimace. "You know, teaching him the fine art of wrangling a few goodies for himself out of the divorce settlement."

Shaking her head, Allie asked, "He ever bother telling this Clara we're not married?"

"That's the best part. Our good pal Billy Stubbs evidently told him we're already married—seeing how it's physically impossible, you know, to have a child any other way."

"Of course," Allie said. "How could I have forgotten?"

Caleb stood at the stove, turning pork chops in his favorite cast-iron skillet. It'd been her father's favorite, too. She hadn't used it since leaving Caleb.

Leaving Caleb....

She rubbed her eyes.

"Tired?" he asked.

"More mental than physical."

"Know what you mean. Wine?" He held up a clear bottle filled with amber liquid, topped by a shiny, twist-off cap.

She laughed.

"Hey," he said. "This was all Adam's doing, not mine."

"Lord help the woman who one day lands him. It'll be grilled cheese and beer all the way."

"Hey, what's wrong with grilled cheese? We used to eat them nearly every day after class."

She wrinkled her nose. "That was before I'd tasted filet."

He glanced at the perfectly browned pork chops in his pan. "Want me to toss these?"

Her stomach growled. "What do you think? I always loved your pork chops."

"Really?"

"Yeah."

"Why didn't you ever say anything?" he asked, stirring the rice simmering in a sauté pan.

"Thought I did."

"Nope." He turned off the flame that'd been steaming broccoli. "Come to think of it, there's a lot you never said."

While he poured "wine" for them both, Allie sighed. "Why do I get the feeling we're not talking about pork chops anymore?"

He shrugged before taking three plates from the cupboard.

"What's on your mind, Caleb? You never were any good at hiding your emotions."

"As opposed to you?"

"Ouch."

"That's one way to describe the way I felt seeing your empty house." He set the plates on the table, following them with napkins and silverware.

"Let's not hash over this again."

"Why?"

"Because it's pointless," she said. "I messed up. I've admitted it. I apologized. What more do you want?"

"Marry me," he blurted.

"What?" Shock spiked her eyebrows.

"The night you told me you were pregnant, Allie, I told you I'd make it right. The night I found out you'd left, I'd been doing just that. Dammit, I was at your house ready to propose."

"Caleb, stop." Hands to her temples, Allie said, "You're not even making sense."

"Like your taking off did? Lying to me did? Us getting married is the only action that would make sense. Our boy needs a dad. You could use help around the house."

"And what do you need, Caleb? What is it you hope to gain from a quickie wedding?"

"Me?" he asked. "I'll finally be getting the son you scammed me out of nine years ago."

"A son? That's it?" Overwhelming sorrow made it hard for Allie to breathe. Wasn't there even a little bit more he wanted from being married to her? Like love? Companionship?

"Isn't Cal enough?" he said. "Nine years ago I told you I'd make things right, and by God, that's what I intend to do."

Tears caught at the back of Allie's throat, stung her eyes. *No, Caleb, making things right wasn't anywhere near good enough nine years ago, and it still isn't now.*

"MAN, THIS IS GOOD," Cal said, digging in to his third pork chop. "How come you guys aren't eating?"

Caleb gulped cheap wine, wishing it was bourbon.

He glanced at Allie, who was picking at her broccoli. She said, "I'm plenty hungry. See?" She forked a miniscule bite.

Caleb rolled his eyes.

"I'm gonna be a vampire for Halloween," Cal said.

"Nice," Caleb said.

Cal beamed upon receiving his father's approval. "Only I'm gonna eat licorice instead of blood. It's still red, but tastes better, don't you think?"

"Absolutely," Allie said. "But wouldn't you rather be something less scary? You know like a scarecrow or Dalmatian? Or that ladybug costume you wore a few years ago? You were so cute."

"Geez, Mom, I don't wanna be *cute*. I wanna be scary. Don't you know anything?"

"Guess not," Allie said, trying to ruffle his hair, but he ducked before she got too close.

"I'm done," he said, guzzling the last of his chocolate milk. "Can I watch Disney Channel?"

"Clear the table first."

"Aw, man."

"Cal," Caleb said reflexively, ignoring Allie's squinty glare.

The boy quickly finished his work, leaving Caleb once again alone with Allie. Only he wasn't all that sure alone with her was a place he wanted to be.

"I'm losing him," she said, cradling her forehead in her hands. "All this macho stuff. Before you showed up, he'd wanted to be an airplane for Halloween."

"Allie," Caleb said, instinctively putting his hand over hers. She tried snatching her hand away but he wouldn't let her. After a few seconds of struggle, she relaxed against him. "He's growing up. It would've happened whether I'd entered the picture or not. Shoot, I remember the year I switched from cute to scary. Same thing happened with my brothers. Gillian even started out as a princess and Cinderella, but wound up a witch." He winced. "Don't tell her I said so, but during a few of her teen years, she kept up the *costume* year-round."

"That's mean." With her free hand, Allie delivered a light smack to his arm. "What about all of Cal's gun play? Before you showed up, he never… How could I have forgotten?"

"What?"

"The day you got here, but before you'd arrived at the courthouse, instead of making airplanes or houses with his Legos, he'd made a gun. This thing with Francis, it's affected him more than I thought. I'm sorry for blaming you."

"Apology accepted," Caleb said, touched by her willingness to admit she'd been wrong. "But even without Francis, Cal is going to grow up. Are you ready? Have you thought about how your life is going to change when he's no longer dependent on you?"

"What's that supposed to mean?"

"I don't know." He shook his head. "I don't even know why I threw it out there."

"To punish me," she said, yanking her hand back, then crossing her arms. "Yet again."

"No."

"Then why do you keep bringing up things you know are only going to upset me?"

"Believe me, Al, if that is what I'm doing, it's not intentional. I'm sorry if you think it has been."

"Are you, Caleb?" The look she fixed on him was chilling. Hard and cold and flinty, and at the same time sad. So sad. Had he caused all that?

"Why, Caleb?" she asked. "Why do you keep asking me to marry you? The truth?"

He rubbed his throbbing temples.

"That's what I thought," she said.

"What? I didn't even say anything." How could he when just looking at her had him so mixed up he could hardly remember his own name, let alone why he was still so angry with her. Why he'd ever been angry with her.

"I'm going to bed," she said. "Could you please tuck in Cal? Oh, and leave the dishes. I'll do them in the morning."

"Allie, wait."

"Why?" She paused on the bottom step of the back staircase, refusing to meet his gaze. "Why should I wait for you now, Caleb, when you never gave me a reason to wait all those years ago?"

"We could start over," he said. "We *should* start over."

"I'm too tired," she said.

"That's not fair."

"To who? Cal or you?"

"Both." He left the table to go to her, finger her robe's soft lapels.

She closed her eyes, arched her head back, giving him an unobstructed view of the sweet, simple column of her throat. His fingertips itched to feel it, caress it. His lips to kiss it.

"Whether you want to acknowledge it or not," he said, "there's still something between us. Just because you abandoned it—me—that doesn't mean the energy went away." Far from it, in his case anyway. While he'd hoped, dreamed, prayed that with time what he felt for Allie would forever fade, in reality it had simmered, just beneath the surface.

Taunting, teasing.

And now it was back.

Reminding him with Allie's every breath just how much he stood to lose all over again if this time he couldn't make her forever his. It wasn't just them he'd be losing, but also their son. A boy who only after knowing a few weeks he already fiercely loved.

Chapter Ten

Caleb avoided Allie as best he could the next few days—tough considering he was being paid to protect her.

At the moment, he was standing outside the Morning Glory Inn, hands shoved in his jeans pockets, yet again trying his damnedest to avoid the inevitable. His only solace was that Allie looked equally uncomfortable, surrounded by his sister, baby niece, brother-in-law and dad. His brother Beau chatted with Adam. His son and stepniece played on a swingset in the two-story inn's side garden. Now that so many of Francis's gang had been rounded up, Caleb's twelve-man team had been slimmed to four.

Allie looked beautiful.

Really extraordinarily beautiful.

The day was sunny and fine, like when they'd been to the petting farm. She wore her long hair down. When the light breeze tickled it against her cheeks, she kept brushing it away. Her denim dress and black boots looked hot. Gillian's baby fisted one of the ends of her orange-and-black scarf, making Allie laugh while his sister passed the baby off to her. Chrissy put the scarf all the way in her mouth, happily gumming the candy-corn decorated silk while the two women talked.

Anger clenched Caleb's gut.

Allie had cheated him out of so much. Out of so many never to be reclaimed moments like seeing her hold their baby. Of sharing holidays with their son and his family. How many different Halloween costumes had he missed?

Chrissy snuggled against Allie's breasts, bringing to mind still more questions. Like had she really asked him to make love to her?

Had he really turned her down?

"What's got you so deep in thought?" his dad asked.

Caleb laughed. "As always—a woman."

"She's a looker, I'll give you that."

"It's not her looks that have me bugged."

"Yep," his dad said. "Gotta say I've had a few angry moments myself over this whole situation. Your boy's handsome. Smart as a whip. Just wish I would've had more time to fish with him or sit with him on my knee."

"I know what you mean."

"So when are you two going to tie the knot?"

"Not sure," Caleb said.

"You asked her though, right?" The sound of Cal's laughter rose above his father's question. Looked like he was having a ball getting to know his cousin, who was currently chasing him, trying to conk him on the head with her fairy princess wand. He took a harmless swing at her with his plastic sword.

"Yes, sir," Caleb said. "But she hasn't given me an answer."

"You planning on keeping after her? Demanding she make a choice?"

"I guess. But unfortunately, we're not living in the old west. I can't just drag her and Cal back to my mountain cabin."

"So then you've put her on a deadline?" his dad asked. "Marry you, or else?"

"Not in so many words, but I think it's understood that as soon as she delivers Francis's sentence, I'm gone—not out of Caleb's life, but hers."

His dad frowned.

"What? I should just hang around like a sap? Waiting for her to make up her mind?"

Shrugging, his dad said, "Got anything better to do?"

"Thanks, Pops. You're a lot of help."

"You're welcome." He winked. "Let me know where to send the bill."

"I SURE APPRECIATE you throwing this party," Allie said to Gillian, early that evening. "I can tell Cal's having a super time."

"What about you?" Gillian asked, making a last-minute repair on a Halloween-themed gingerbread haunted castle she and Meghan had spent the past week perfecting for the party. Allie had been under the impression that they were just going to have an intimate get together for family, but Gillian had instead hired a party planner who had transformed the inn's event room into a spooky wonderland complete with carnival games that Cal and his cousin were happily trying to win. Piles of candy, and howling coyote and cackling witch sound effects were also crowd pleasers.

Cal's entire class was invited, along with all of Allie's co-workers. Allie told Giselle Caleb was officially off-limits—not that Allie yet knew what she'd do with him, but the point was to keep her options open. Giselle now used her many charms on Bear, who stoically stood guard near the door. Though his arms were crossed, face grim and alert, Giselle looked determined to make him smile.

Allie's mom hadn't been able to come. Turns out she'd promised to dog sit for neighbors who were taking a twenty-five-year wedding anniversary cruise. While Allie missed her mom, she was secretly relieved to put off at least her portion of the family reunion.

Allie had been touched by Gillian's gesture to throw the party. Touched, but also confused. Why would Caleb's sister do all of this for her and her son? Especially after she'd kept Cal from the Logues for all these years?

"Sure, I'm, ah, having lots of fun." Allie flashed Gillian a hesitant smile.

"Look," Gillian said, licking black frosting from her thumb, "before all of Cal's friends get here, there's something I need to get off my chest. Let's talk."

"Here it comes," Allie said with a grimace in a relatively quiet corner near Coyote Mountain Slide, which was not yet in use. "I've been wondering when you'd let me have it."

"Oh, Allie, no." Gillian surprised her with a hug. "Where would you get that idea?"

"Maybe because that's what I'd do if I were standing in your shoes?"

"Yell at yourself?" Gillian laughed. "What purpose would that serve?"

Tears sprung to Allie's eyes. "Oh, Gillian, I'm so sorry for what I've done. At the time, it just—I couldn't see any other option. Caleb had so many plans, all of which centered around a career that could snatch him from me and our son. I never meant to lie about Cal. It just happened. Every year, I planned on telling him, but the more time that went by, the more scared I got. I didn't know how he'd react. Couldn't imagine."

"Shh…" Gillian said, patting Allie's back. "Now that you and my brother are finally getting married, you can put all that behind you. Yes, you hurt him—all of us—but we're a forgiving bunch."

Allie nodded.

"Whoa," Gillian asked when Allie couldn't stop crying. "What's the matter now?"

"N-nothing," Allie said with a sniffle.

"You and my brother *are* getting married?"

"I—I don't know."

"He asked, didn't he?" Gillian demanded to know.

"Uh-huh."

"Then what's the problem?" Scooping up a handful of M&Ms, Gillian popped a few into her mouth and chewed.

Sighing, Allie asked, "Got a few years?"

"Honey, after what Joe and I went through to get together, I know what you mean. How about you and I trade our punch for wine and head upstairs for some serious girl talk. The boys can handle the party."

"You think?" Glancing at the four rowdy kids already assembled, Allie had a tough time imagining Caleb handling even them, let alone more.

"Oh, sure. Joe's great with kids, and it's high time my brother learned."

CALEB FLASHED a panicked look at his brother-in-law, Joe. "Where'd that wife of yours run off to?"

"She said she and your soon-to-be-wife were just going for one *quick* glass of wine. Next thing I knew, you and me were both banished to kid hell."

Laughing, Caleb yanked a Power Ranger off of the snack table.

After corralling a daisy, a vampire and Miss America, then finding time to snag a few hot dogs, Caleb was hiding out with Joe in the haunted house when he asked, "How long did it take for Gillian to give you an answer after you proposed?"

"About two-point-five seconds once I got my head out of my behind enough to get up the nerve to ask. Why?"

"No biggee," Caleb said around his latest bite of hot dog.

"All right, Gil's gonna kill me if I don't ask the obvious question."

"What's that?"

"Well?" Joe peeled the foil from a chocolate cupcake. "What's the problem? We've all been planning a Christmas wedding. Should I make your sister cool her matchmaking heels?"

Rolling his eyes, Caleb said, "You should know better than anyone that you can't make Gillian do anything."

"True," Joe said. "Hey, you know that kid?"

"Which one?" Caleb leaned to his right, peering out the crooked haunted house window.

"The one with the pink hair and spiders for eyelashes who's fishing in the punch fountain?"

"Sure. That'd be my son's *pal* Billy Stubbs. Save my spot while I feed him to the werewolves."

"TIRED?" Caleb asked Allie after they'd said goodbye to the last little goblin.

"Mmm-hmm…" She eased her arm around his waist, resting her head on his shoulder. It was such a simple gesture. One that in the grand scheme of things probably meant nothing, but he couldn't help but feel a stir of hope.

"Judging by the size of Cal's grin when he took off with Reider and Sam, I'd say the night was a complete success." Because of minimal risk, Caleb agreed to the sleepover under the condition that Sam's home had been previously surveyed for potential security weaknesses, and the boy had been accompanied by a security team. His parents had also been apprised of the still potentially dangerous situation, as had all of the parents of the children who'd attended the party.

"Thanks," Allie said to Gillian and Joe. "I can't get over how much trouble you all went to in welcoming Cal into your family."

"Sure," they said in unison.

The couple stood with their arms around each other, occasionally sharing glances that told anyone looking they'd found what it sometimes felt like the whole rest of the world was seeking—love.

Gillian said, "Don't forget, tonight was also about welcoming *you* into our family. You've just gotta remember to—" She leaned over to Allie, whispering into her ear.

Allie busted into the kind of laughter Caleb hadn't heard coming from her in years. "Will do."

"What was that about?" Caleb asked Joe.

"I'm too tired to decode it tonight. Come on," he said to his wife, taking her by the hand to tug her toward the stairs. "You're going to bed—with me."

"Yes, sir," she said, but not without an over-the-shoulder grin to Allie.

After they'd left, Caleb said, "Spill it."

"What?" She batted her eyelashes.

The marshal on duty with them at the far end of the inn's lobby cleared his throat. "Should I, ah, give you two some privacy?"

"Thanks, Kent." Damn. Caleb had forgotten he was even there. "But Allie and I were just leaving."

"We were?" she asked, at it again with those flirty eyelashes, adding a pout to her uncharacteristic sex-kitten routine.

"You been drinking?" he asked.

"Just a smidge."

"That why you left chaperoning the party to me and Joe?"

"Maybe," she said, toying with one of the buttons on his shirt.

"What the hell are you up to?" he asked, using a lock of her hair to tweak the end of her nose.

She wagged a hotel key at him.

Again, Caleb was left groaning. "What exactly have you and my sister been talking about?"

"You know." Wink, wink. "Girl stuff."

"No, I don't know," he said, taking the key and putting his hand on the small of her back to lead her up the stairs. "How 'bout you tell me."

They'd been in the room exactly forty-five minutes—long enough for room service to deliver wine and hot artichoke dip—when Allie fell asleep.

Caleb sighed.

Whatever Allie and his sister had gabbed about, it looked like it'd be morning till he and Al got a chance to talk.

He took off his roommate's boots and scarf, then tucked her in for the night. But it was only nine-thirty and he was still wide-awake, so he made a quick call to both security teams to make sure all was still well, then headed down to the inn's small bar in hopes of finding his dad and brothers.

"HEY THERE, SLEEPY HEAD," Caleb said to Allie the next morning in their suite. He'd been reading the paper at a small table in front of a large bank of windows. If he'd opened the shades, no doubt sunshine would've flooded the room. But until Allie and Cal were one hundred percent out of danger, he saw no sense in tempting fate. "I ordered breakfast. A little of everything."

"Thanks." She sat up only to clutch her stomach and forehead. "Whoa. How much wine did your sister and I drink?"

"Considering the fact that you, and according to

Joe—Gillian—were both out by nine-thirty, I'd say you both had more vino than you thought." He went to her, perching on the side of the bed. "Need anything? Aspirin? A cool cloth?"

"Yes, please. To both." She grimaced. "And while you're at it, how about a new head?"

"Will do."

In a few minutes, he was back with both items, along with a cold can of Sprite. He opened it for her to help wash down the two white tablets.

When she'd finished, he took the can, setting it on the bedside table. "I don't know about you," he said, "but that was one of the most romantic nights of my life."

While he settled on his side of the bed, bunching the pillows behind him, she stuck out her tongue.

He sighed. "Remind me to let my sister have it next time we see her."

"She was only trying to help."

"By getting you sloshed?"

Allie rolled her eyes. "I would hardly call a few glasses of wine *sloshed*. I'm just not used to drinking, that's all."

"I know," he said, cupping his hand to her sick belly. "I'm just messing with you. Wouldn't have even mattered if you were awake. Remember? How my job kind of makes you off-limits? I shouldn't even kiss you, let alone want to do way more."

He tried lifting his hand, but she put hers on top of his.

"Stay." She swallowed hard. "One of the things your

sister and I talked about was me being more open. Not only with myself, but you."

"Oh?"

Half laughing and shaking her head, she said, "I've made such a mess of things."

"I'd say we both have."

Hand still over his, she said, "Right here—now—let's start fresh."

"Nothing would make me happier."

Leaning close, she kissed him. Softly, sweetly, as if maybe it were for the first time all over again.

"When I was pregnant," she said, her cheek against his, her body against his, her soul too close to his for anything but truth, "I missed you so bad. I lost count of the number of times I almost called you. I used to fall asleep cupping my hands to our baby, wishing they were your hands. Praying they were your hands." Tears streamed down her cheeks.

"Geez, Al, all it would've taken was one call. Hell, I tried finding you, but your mother told me you didn't want to be found."

"I know," she said. "I was so young. Proud. Stupid."

"And now?" he asked, almost afraid to.

"Now, I'd like a second chance. I'm begging for a second chance. But I can't just marry you in a quickie wedding. It's been so long, Caleb. I need to know these feelings between us are real. Yes, Cal needs a father. And I would never again in a million, trillion years deny you, or your family, another moment with him. In fact, if for some reason you should decide marriage isn't in the cards for us, I would explore finding a bench closer to Portland so that you and Cal could be to-gether."

"You'd do that?" he asked. "For me?"

She nodded. "Considering the years I took from the two of you—yes. It's the least I can do to make amends."

Caleb released a gush of air he hadn't realized he'd been holding. What could've caused this sudden turn-around in Allie's stand on their relationship—or lack thereof? "What exactly did my sister say to you last night?"

Chapter Eleven

Lips curving into a brilliant smile, Allie said, "It wasn't so much what she said to me, but what she showed me. We looked through photo albums of your family. In them there were so many wonderful shots of Gillian and Joe and the life they share. But there were also a lot of you playing with your nieces. Of all of you hamming it up on family ski trips and sitting around the table at Thanksgiving and Christmas. It made me see how much Cal and I are missing by not being part of all that. And not just us, but my mom, too. It's been only the three of us for as long as I can remember. Sitting around her big empty dining room table at holidays. Only having a roasting hen because there aren't enough of us to justify a whole turkey or ham."

Caleb pulled her in for a hug. He rolled onto his back, lifting her on top of him, sliding his fingers deep into her hair.

Over the past nine years, they'd both missed so much—but no more. Starting today, this second, neither of them was ever going to miss out on anything again.

AT SCHOOL ON MONDAY, Cal couldn't stop smiling. This had been the best Halloween *ever*. He loved his new uncles and grandfather and aunt and cousins, and man, if he could have any wish in the world, it'd be to live with all of his new, big family forever.

But back at Reider's house after the party, he'd IM'd Clara, and she said that unless his mom and dad got married, he wouldn't ever get to see his new family 'cept for sometimes on weekends and during summer vacation. Well, that just wasn't enough. Which was why he was now hungry—because he'd had to pay Clara his lunch money for her to tell him how to get his mom and dad married.

"Want my cookie?" Sam asked.

"You sure you don't want it?" Cal asked.

"Nah. Reider gave me his 'cause he's allergic to raisins."

"Oh. Then, yeah. Thanks. Got any paper?"

"Uh-uh," Sam said. "It's all in my desk. Why do you need it?"

"I gotta meet Clara at recess. She made me pay her my lunch money to tell me how to get Mom and Dad married."

"Man," Sam said. "For that much money, she should hafta write it down for you."

ON THE BENCH, presiding over the tedious jury selection for a copyright infringement complaint, Allie tried focusing, but it was tough getting past giddy teenaged pangs of wanting to hurry up and finish with work so she could get home to see Caleb, who was spending the day with Cal at his school.

It'd only been a day since they'd shared that precious Saturday morning at the inn, but already she was eager to explore more of their burgeoning romance.

"Thanks, guys," she said to her security team once she'd finally adjourned for the day. All had been so calm since the end of Francis's trial, so she didn't really see why their presence was even necessary, but if it kept Caleb close to her, she wasn't about to complain.

"Sure. No biggee," Adam said, glancing over his shoulder, then muttering something into his radio microphone.

"Nice job on the job," Kent, one of the more stone-faced marshals, said in the hall. He wasn't a very talkative guy, so from him, Allie took this as high praise… Although odd, considering the afternoon's monotonous work.

"All's clear," Adam said. "Let's rock and roll."

"After you," Kent said, opening Allie's office door only to step back and let her go in first, instead of entering, checking that the coast was clear, then letting her in. She was still pondering the change in tradition when she opened her mouth, then put her hand over it to contain the unjudgelike whoop of glee that would've escaped.

Standing in the center of a jumble of tarp-covered furniture were two very green marshals, holding green paintbrushes. Her formerly yellowed walls were now a vibrant shade of jungle-green.

"Taa-daa!" Caleb said. "This better?"

"Better?" she squealed, running to him for a hug—

not caring if in the process he got green paint on her solemn black robe. "It's awesome! Thank you!" She pulled back. "But I thought you were on duty and spent the day with Cal at school?"

He grinned. "With your observational skills, it's a good thing I'm the protector and you're the protectee. Relax. According to the last report, our son is out of class for the day and seated at the kitchen table doing homework."

She rolled her eyes.

"I'm gonna go clean up," Bear said. "And for the record, I'm all paid up on returned favors."

Before the huge, sweet lug of a marshal got away, Allie squeezed him in a heartfelt hug as well. "Thanks. I love it."

"Sure," Bear said, hugging her back.

"And I also love the spot of green on your head," she teased. "Might be a whole new fashion statement for you."

He growled.

"I'll be outside if you need me," Adam said. "Kent wants me to introduce him to that hottie in the front office."

"Go for it, man," Caleb said. "She's a looker."

"Hey," Allie said, swatting his arm. "Watch it. I'll hold you in contempt."

"Mmm…" He tugged her back against him. "Being locked in a cell with you doesn't sound all that bad."

That earned him another swat. "Seriously, Caleb, this goes beyond sweet. I can't believe you even remembered me telling you how uninspiring this office was, let alone that you took it upon yourself to paint it for me. How can I thank you?"

"Boy," he said, scratching his head. "That's a tough question. I would ask for a kiss, but…."

But she was already on her tiptoes, kissing him, molding her lips to his, parting them with her tongue. He tilted his head and groaned, inviting her farther in.

He backed up, taking her along with him, eventually landing them against a tarp-covered table. Unfortunately, under their weight, it skidded out from under them.

Allie shrieked as they went down, but Caleb was there, cushioning her fall.

The door burst open. Adam blurted, "You all right?"

Allie, straddling Caleb, felt her face turning a hundred shades of red.

"We're, ah, good," Caleb said. "Thanks."

"You'd better be damned glad your boyfriend's my brother," Adam said with a huge grin, at the same time wagging his index finger. "Otherwise I'd report you for mugging a marshal." Just as abruptly as he'd entered, he left.

"Ugh," Allie said, dropping her chin on Caleb's chest. "That couldn't have been any more humiliating."

Sliding his hand from the small of her back down to her rear end, he said, "You saying you're embarrassed to be seen with me?"

"Seen *riding* you in my office—yeah. I find that a little humbling, considering the rather public state of my career."

"You can count on Adam to keep your dirty little secret."

"*My* dirty secret?" she said, laughing and pummeling his chest. "What about you? You started this."

"Um, for the record…" He cleared his throat. "I was innocently painting your office, when you virtually threw yourself at me. I was only trying to fend you off when—"

Before any additional verbal bologna spilled past his gorgeous lips, she kissed them good and hard. And just in case he got any big ideas about starting back up with his teasing, she kissed him again softly. Melting against him until he was rolling them over, putting himself on top. Judging by the all-male pulsing bulge against her midsection, there was no question that he wouldn't have had a problem taking things still further. At least until he pushed himself up and off of her, swiping his fingers through his hair.

"Damn," he said. "You don't kiss anyone else like that, do you?"

"What if I did?" she asked with a sassy smile.

He smiled back—sort of. Only she couldn't tell if it was a "ha-ha" smile, or maybe, a "just a little bit serious" smile. "If you did," he said, "no question about it, the guy kissing you back would have to be taught a lesson in trespassing."

"COME ON, COME ON," Allie's son said, dragging her by her hand through the open back door and into the house. Caleb was behind her. "Geez, what took you guys so long?"

Feeling a blush rise, once they all stood inside, Allie turned to Caleb. "How about you tell Cal what took so long."

"Well, bud, it was like this…" Caleb took a seat on one of the counter stools. "Me and Bear painted your mom's office, but—"

"Cool! What color?"

"Green, but—"

"Okay, come see what I made for you guys. You're going on a date."

A date?

Not that Allie wouldn't enjoy doing just that, but since when did Cal even know the word *date,* let alone what a couple was supposed to do on one?

This time, Cal dragged Caleb along after him toward the dining room.

"Taa-daa!" their little boy said. "You like it?"

The dining room table had been set with the paint-stained plastic cloth she and Cal used for crafts. On top of that sat mismatched place settings of her grandmother's white china plates and the heavier, everyday cobalt blue saucers, bowls and mugs. Filling all the dishes was an assortment of clumped macaroni and cheese that looked like it hadn't been cooked—probably an accurate assumption since Cal wasn't yet allowed to use the stove. Then there was applesauce and sliced apples. Cookies and peanut butter sandwiches. Chocolate milk in the mugs, and what looked like turquoise Kool-Aid in the martini glasses she'd purchased for a holiday office party and hadn't used since. In the center of the table sat her best crystal vase—another gift from her grandmother. Filling the vase was water and a burgundy plastic poinsettia left over from the previous year's Christmas.

"This is amazing, man." Caleb whistled, giving his son's back a pat. "Other than our date, what's the occasion? Is it my birthday and I forgot?"

"No," Cal said with a giggle. "At least I don't think so."

"But it could be?" Caleb asked.

"No, it couldn't," Allie said, pulling her son over for a hug.

"How do you know?" Cal asked.

"Because I happen to know for a fact your father's birthday is in March."

"Sorry," Cal said, his expression highly serious. "Want me to write it down for you so you don't forget?"

"Thanks," Caleb said. "That'd be great."

"Okay, but first, you guys have to sit."

"What about you?" Allie asked while her suspiciously well-mannered son pulled out her chair.

"I already ate," he said, heading around the table to pull out his father's chair as well. "You guys go ahead. Oh, and since I'm not allowed to play with matches, here." He handed her the big pack of wooden kitchen matches. "You can light the candles."

"Thank you," she said, solemnly taking them from him.

"You're welcome. Bye. Have fun!"

"But, what're you—" Too late, judging by the clomps up the stairs—he was already heading for his room. A few seconds after that, faint tinny pop music pulsed through the dining room ceiling.

"Is it just me?" she asked, putting her crumpled red napkin—also left over from last Christmas—on her lap. "Or is this whole setup a little suspicious?"

"You think?" Caleb dug in to his saucer of applesauce.

"Who do you think put him up to this?"

"If I had to guess," he said, guzzling his chocolate milk, "this plot reeks of Clara."

"Wow, GUYS," Allie said a few days later in her home's detached garage. "This is like the rooster Taj Mahal."

Cal grinned with pride, pounding a nail into the coop's shingles.

Caleb said, "A couple of off duty guys chipped in to help fence a back corner of the yard. So once we get this done, we should be good to go."

"Will you take me to see it?" Allie asked her security team.

Caleb glanced toward the garage windows. They were covered in brown paper. "If you don't mind, I'd rather keep you both inside."

"But why?" she asked. "You said yourself that most likely Cal and I are out of danger."

He shrugged.

While Cal was busy pounding another nail, Allie gestured for Caleb to join her alongside the tool bench.

"What's up?" he asked.

"You tell me. Is there something going on I should know about?"

He looked away.

"Caleb?"

"Look," he said, taking her hand, brushing her palm with his thumb, in the process sending unexpected pleasure deep into her belly. "There's nothing concrete. Just a gut feeling that we're in the eye of the storm."

She took his free hand, gave him a squeeze. "I appreciate that you care, but really, my gut feeling is that we're fine."

Sighing, he pulled her into his arms.

"What?" she said against his chest. "Haven't you ever heard of women's intuition?"

"Have I told you lately you make me crazy?"

"Hmm…" She put her finger to her lips. "Not that I remember, but I've been awfully busy. I suppose I might've forgotten any specific statement alluding to that intent."

"Mom?" Cal asked. "Since you and Caleb are hugging and laughing and stuff, does that mean you're getting married? 'Cause my friend Clara said that's what you have to do."

Allie made the mistake of looking up at Caleb to see the smile lighting his eyes. It said, "Hey, I answered the 'Why We Were Late Coming Home From the Courthouse' question. This one's all yours."

"Is that what you want?" Allie asked. "For your father and I to get married?"

He jiggled the nails in his right hand. "I dunno."

"Well, I kind of think judging by the fancy meal you fixed the other night, then by your question now, this is at least a subject you've thought about."

Looking at his father, Cal whined, "Can we get back to building? All this talking about girl stuff is boring."

Allie had to bite her lip to keep from laughing.

"Sure, bud," Caleb said. "Is your mom allowed to stay, or is hammering too manly for her?"

"Well…" Cal took a good, long while to ponder the question. "I suppose if she doesn't tell us to be careful and stuff it'd be all right if she stays."

"Gee, thanks." Allie cast them both a pouty grin. "I can tell I'm loved."

"We love you, Mom. We just don't need you getting in the way of construction."

"Yeah," Caleb said with a broad wink. "We can't have you getting in the way."

Allie took a folding chair from its canvas storage bag, then set up camp at what she hoped was a safe distance from all the manly banging. She didn't think she could ever be a safe distance from Caleb's broad shoulders, or the honed muscles of his forearms and biceps, show-cased as he wielded his hammer. Maybe even more disconcerting was the sight of him curved around their son, helping him position a shingle, or yank out a crooked nail.

We love you, Mom.

She knew her son loved her, but what about Caleb?

From all that he'd shared about what he'd been feeling the last time they'd seen each other, she feared her mistake of ever leaving him was more in the realm of tragedy. That maybe—no, almost certainly—Caleb *had* loved her. *Would've* married her. If only she'd stayed around long enough for him to ask.

But then really, what good would that have done?

Sure, they'd have been married, raising Cal together,

but ultimately, marriage wouldn't have kept Caleb from entering the marshal's service.

Cal erupted in laughter.

She looked up.

Father and son fought an epic mini-sword fight with nails.

Allie's first instinct was to leap from her chair and make them stop before someone got hurt. But realistically, aside from a possible minor scratch, the worst harm that could come to her son was maybe a sore tummy from too much laughing.

How many times in the past had she dealt with the tough single-parent issue of there not being nearly enough hours in the day for her to even do the necessities for Cal, let alone squeeze in extras like goofy play?

But seeing him now, out of breath with laughter, was play really something extra? Or was it as vital to a child's life as clean water and air?

In that moment, seeing the joy on her son's face, the full impact of what she'd done by not telling Caleb the truth about their son's existence hit her in a crushing blow. Her chest ached from the weight of it.

Not wanting either of her men to see her tears, she got up from her chair as quickly as possible and went to stand outside.

Just beyond the reach of the back porch floodlight, the night was cold and dark and it was drizzling, only she didn't care, because that's how she felt inside.

She'd been so concerned about protecting her son from all things that *might've* happened if Caleb got hurt, she'd missed the bigger picture. How she cherished memories of time spent with her father, as Cal would with his.

"I thought you were in the house." Caleb said, stepping outside the garage. "You should've waited for an escort."

Sniffling, she shook her head.

"Do any of my guys even know you're out here?"

"Oh, Caleb, stop it with the security thing, okay? I'm fine. Cal's fine. You caught the bad guys. We're all fine."

"Are we?"

Gripping her shoulders, he turned her to face him.

The drizzle turned to rain.

"I—I don't know what you mean"

With the pads of his thumbs, he softly swept the shadows beneath her eyes. "You've been crying."

Again, she shook her head.

"You're not mad about all that stupid macho crap Cal said back there?"

"No. As usual, you were right. He probably could use a little manly influence in his life."

"Then what's the problem?"

Like she seemed to be doing a lot lately, she threw her arms around him, hugging him like she'd never let go. "I'm sorry," she said. "Please forgive me for keeping him from you for so long. He needs you. I've done a terrible job. He shouldn't know how to knit. My mother and I have turned him into some freak of nature."

"No, no," Caleb said, easing his hand beneath her sweater's hem, then smoothing his strong, warm fingers up and down her back. "Every guy should know how

to knit. I'm sure it might really come in handy for…"
He laughed. "Well, I'm not sure for what, but baby,
Cal's okay. He's an awesome kid. He's got a damned
strong foundation, and he got it from you." Hands cradling either side of her face, he tilted her head, forcing
her to look at him, to catch the full weight of his words.
"Yeah, I'd give anything to have been here from the start
with you, helping to shape his life and views. But I'm
here now, and I thought we'd decided that's what matters."

"It is." She sniffed.

"All right, then. No more tears. Let me get Bear in
the garage to help Cal finish the roof, then we'll get you
inside for a hot bath."

"No, wait," she said, wearing what she hoped was a
big grin that might even rival the size of one of Caleb's.
"Maybe I'd rather have Bear helping me?"

"Ha, ha," Caleb said. "Get that sassy mouth of
yours upstairs and in the tub. I'll be up to deal with
you momentarily."

Chapter Twelve

With Cal squared away with Bear in the garage, Caleb stood outside Allie's bedroom door, palms sweating, pulse pounding as if he were setting off on his first date.

He wasn't on duty, but that didn't erase the moral dilemma of what he wanted so desperately to do.

Was he just supposed to bust through the doors and pull some macho stunt like *taking* her on the side of the tub? Should he pull the nice guy routine and allow Allie to finish her bath in private? Did he go in and just pretend to be comfortable sitting on the small ottoman Allie used for putting on her makeup? Did he sit there, butt half-on/half-off the ridiculous, spindly thing, trying to keep up casual conversation when all he wanted to do was—

Just thinking of Allie lying there all naked and soapy and slick....

He adjusted his fly.

On one hand, she was the mother of his child, and as such, should be treated with a certain amount of respect.

On the other hand, she was hot. He'd never even

seen her pregnant. She could've been with another guy. How did he even know Cal was his?

He scowled.

He knew, because he *knew*.

Because his heart told him so every time he looked in the kid's eyes, the same shade as his.

Pacing the not nearly long enough hall, Caleb rubbed his forehead. What to do? What to do?

Manly choice—bust down the door and take everything he wanted.

Gentlemanly choice, ethical choice—go downstairs and crash in front of ESPN.

The bedroom door creaked open.

"Well?" Allie asked, looking all pink and fresh-scrubbed and so beautiful she took his breath away. "You planning on standing out here all night?"

"You didn't stay long in the tub," he said, his voice more husky than usual.

"I got the water too hot. Started feeling more like I was boiling than bathing."

He chuckled.

She giggled.

The implication of what could've happened between them if only she'd stayed in the water hung in the air.

"Is Cal almost finished in the garage?" she asked.

"Yeah. If it's all right with you, I thought we might head back to the petting zoo this weekend to pick out a rooster and hens. Maybe chicks."

"Sure," she said. "Hens. Chicks. Either way, sounds good."

"The kid also needs a horse."

"A horse?" She raised her eyebrows. "And which *kid* would that be for?"

"I'm hurt," he said, clutching his chest. "Are you intimating I'm trying to fast-track my son's appreciation for all things having to do with the Old West by buying him a horse?"

"Maybe that's what I'm saying."

"Okay, but now that you know what I'm up to," he said, "does this mean it's a go for the horse? Because if so, the same guy who's selling us the rooster has a great little paint that—"

"I'm sorry, Caleb, but no. First off, we don't have enough land, and second, who's going to take care of it when you're gone?"

"Cal," he said. "Besides which, what if I'm not gone?"

"You mean what if we get married? Isn't that an awfully big 'what if' considering the fact you apparently don't even want to—" *Make love to me.*

"Case closed on the horse," he said, sharply looking away. "Anyway, I was just messing around."

"Sure," she said. "I kind of figured as much."

"I know," he said.

"Um-hmm."

Shifting his weight from one foot to the other, Caleb sighed. "What are we doing?"

"What do you mean?" she asked, knowing full well they were doing a pretty impressive tap dance. And it had nothing to do with a horse! Like the night she'd flat-out begged him to make love to her, but he'd turned her down. And the night Gillian bought them a romantic night at the Inn that was supposed to have rekindled their romance, but didn't work out that way. The love-making that used to come so naturally between them wasn't happening.

Why? Was it just one more sign they weren't meant to be married?

"Geez, Al, I'd planned to barge right into that bath-room and plunder you, but until this case is officially over…."

"I know," she said, bowing her head. "I feel the same. I want whatever we used to have to come back, but…."

"You're scared it's been so long that the magic we shared is gone?"

"Pretty much," she said. "I guess that's it."

"Yeah," he said. "Me, too."

He reached for her hand, did that nifty trick where he swirled his finger round and round her palm.

She swallowed hard, desperately searching for air past distracting rising heat.

He raised her fevered palm to his lips. Strong firm lips that made her mouth jealous of her hand. His moist breath tickled, but this was no laughing matter. Instant arousal licked her belly. Her nipples puckered and hardened.

That magic? In her case anyway, it was there.

Times ten!

Eyes closed, she focused on her next hitched breath.

"Want to go downstairs?" he asked. "See if Adam left any ice cream?"

She shook her head, then nodded.

"Yeah," Caleb said. "Me, too."

"You two are up awfully early," Allie said the next morning. Her eyes were barely open, yet here were her two men, hard at work in the kitchen.

"We're cookin' breakfast," Cal said.

"I see that." She had a seat at one of the counter bar stools. "What's the occasion?"

"Nothing special," Caleb said, flipping an egg, then stirring oatmeal. "Just thought you deserved a break." He shot a sexy grin over his shoulder.

"Thanks," she said, more than a little flustered.

"You're welcome," Cal said, thankfully having missed the undercurrent flowing between his mom and dad. The one that ran full of hope that maybe, just maybe, if the stars aligned and they played their cards right and all that other sappy stuff fools say when they're wishing for their wildest dreams to come true, she just might get her perfect family after all.

"Caleb," Allie complained when he presented her with the lunch he'd brought her. "You've got to stop being so nice."

"This beats all." Laughing, he pulled out a chair at her office table, spun it around, then straddled it, resting his arms on the chair's back. "I can't believe you're complaining about me doing something nice. Oh, and before I forget, I brought this, too. Found it at a yard sale down the street from the house." From his coat pocket he took a barely eight-inch-tall porcelain figurine of a hula dancer doing her thing under a swaying palm. Handing it to Allie, he said, "I know she's probably tacky, but I liked the expression on her face.

Thought it might relax you. You know, looking at her and the tree and thinking of someplace warm and sunny. Plus, the green goes with your office."

Allie, beaming, gingerly took the dancer. "You don't have to do a sell job. She's adorable." Already up from the table, she set the dancer on her desk. "Perfect," she said, heading back his way to land a kiss to his cheek.

"That's all I get for bringing lunch and a present?"

She tried again, this time aiming for his lips.

Caleb slipped his hand along her soft cheek, going farther to bury his fingers in even softer hair. He wasn't sure who'd come up with the bright idea of including a little tongue but he liked it. A lot. Maybe too much judging by the tent being pitched in his pants.

"Whew," she said, eventually pulling back. "Maybe you should bring lunch and a present every day." She winked. "That way I get to thank you every day."

He winked back. "Sounds like a plan to me." After eating for a few minutes in companionable silence, he asked, "So you really like the knickknack? 'Cause if you don't, I can—"

"Don't you dare do anything with her," Allie said, stealing one of his barbecue chips.

"I saw that."

She made a face.

"Cal says you have a thing about clutter, so I don't want you feeling like with all the stuff I drag in, I'm ruining your space."

"I don't for a minute think that," she said, covering his hand. "I love everything you've brought. The Mr. Chia Head and canisters and the palm and all the movie magazines and Jolly Ranchers you keep bringing—and especially the totem pole thingee. Every bit of it is quirky and cute and wonderful…. Kind of like the man who brought them."

Damn if her speech didn't have him feeling a little misty behind his eyes. "Thanks," he managed.

"For what? I'm thanking you."

"Yeah, well…" He shrugged. "Just thanks. This has been the nicest assignment I've had in a while. Doesn't really even feel like work—being around you, I mean."

"Gee, thanks," Allie said. "I think."

SINCE CALEB had to catch up on paperwork, Bear and Adam took Allie home that afternoon from the court-house.

Cal and his security detail were at his friend Reider's, leaving Allie on her own. She popped a roasting hen in the oven, added a few scrubbed, foil-wrapped potatoes, then tossed a salad.

Seeing how that had taken all of fifteen minutes, and for once she was caught up on all of her court document reading, she was left in the unfamiliar territory of having nothing to do.

She went upstairs to check the hampers, thinking she might as well get a head start on the weekend wash. While passing by Caleb's room, she noticed a pile of dirty clothes in the corner by the closet. Figuring he probably needed clean clothes worse than Cal or her, she scooped them up, then headed to the basement laundry room.

On top of the pile was that denim shirt Caleb was always wearing that had the missing button.

Aside from that shirt, she loaded the rest of his clothes, then trekked back upstairs to fetch her sewing basket from the hall closet.

Since she still wasn't *allowed* to open curtains or blinds, she headed for the den where the windows were too high to need blinds, but in the late afternoon, sunlight still streamed through.

Curled up in an armchair, Caleb's masculine scent wreathed every tug of the needle while she sewed a new button on his shirt.

It was such a simple thing—sewing on a button—yet Caleb was always doing such nice things for her she wanted to do more for him. She wanted to do everything for him. Cook delicious meals that made his stomach happy. Iron his always wrinkled white shirts. Massage his shoulders and feet. Kiss him and hug him and buy him that horse he wanted.

She wanted to do all that, but should she?

For whatever reason, he wasn't ready to take their relationship much past the status of kissing friends.

Funny, how he'd asked her to marry him, but not to sleep with him. Funny and refreshing. Kind of upside down in times of commonplace one-night stands.

Was Caleb's lack of physical affection merely like he said—an issue of work ethics and respect? Or could it be something more? Like him not even being attracted to her?

Nine years was a long time.

People changed. As did their tastes.

What if she was no longer his type? And he was just kissing her to be polite?

What if he didn't like the few pounds she'd added or the occasional gray hairs that had started popping up?

Just thinking about him coming home soon filled her with giddy excitement. Did he feel the same about coming home to her? Cal, yes. But *her?* The woman who might become his wife?

Putting down the shirt, she headed to a decorative mirror on the den's far wall, searching, searching for some particularly unattractive portion of herself she might've missed.

There was a new mole on her left cheek. At her last physical, her doctor said it wasn't any big deal, but maybe she should just go ahead and have it removed? Her eyebrows were totally out of control. How long had it been since she'd had time for a professional wax? And then there was—

"Like what you see?" Caleb asked, humor in his tone.

She jumped, put her hand to her chest before spinning around. "Couldn't you have at least knocked?"

"Sorry," he said, giving the nearest wall a few thumps. "May I come in?"

"No," she said. "I'm mad at you."

"How come?" He crossed the room, fitting his arms around her hips, lacing his fingers proprietarily low.

"I'm not sure," she said. "Just because."

"Oh," he said, nodding his head wisely. "Sounds like a typical female reason to me."

He was just going in for a kiss when she blurted, "Caleb? Do you still find me attractive?"

"Huh?"

"You know, in your eyes, am I still pretty?"

"Woman," he said in a throaty growl, "you're beyond attractive and deep into the realm of goddess territory."

She rolled her eyes. "You trying to butter me up to sell me a nice tract of swamp land?"

"Nah," he said. "Just trying to squelch whatever crazy fear I saw in your eyes before you even knew I was here, while at the same time butter you up."

"Butter me up for what?"

"Oh, I don't know," he said with a big grin. "How about we just mosey on into the kitchen and you can see for yourself."

"CALEB! IT'S BEAUTIFUL…" Allie scratched her head, scrunched her nose. "But, um, what is it?" Standing at least six feet tall in front of the closed kitchen window blinds was an exotic-stemmed orange flower.

"You're not seeing it at the right angle," he said. "Here…" He turned it around, so she could view it from the front.

"It's a bookshelf," she said with an excited clap. On the other side of the first flower, there was an identical one. The two formed supports for the shelves lining the center. "I love it! Where did you find it?"

"You know how I like yard sales?"

"No-oo-o," she said with an exaggerated sigh and grin. "I never would've guessed that about you."

"Anyway…" He shot her a look. "On the way to the courthouse this afternoon, I stopped off at a yard sale. The guy was a weekend artist. Makes these things to sell at craft fairs. I thought it might be pretty in your bedroom. It's still a little plain in there. Plus—" he looked away and grinned "—guess you could use something to store all the stuff I've dragged in."

"Okay, but wait," she said. "You think my gorgeous, minimalist bedroom is *plain?*"

"Yeah. It is."

"And so you've appointed yourself my official redecorator?"

"Um-hmm." With his sleeve, he dusted the flower's upper shelf.

Crossing her arms, she couldn't help but smile. "Well, if the rest of your work is as great as this, I just might keep you on for a good long while."

She'd meant the statement as a joke, but just as she'd caught the unintentional double entendre, the slight catch in Caleb's breath said he hadn't missed it, either.

A good long while, as in marriage.

They'd had so much fun the past few days. Would a whole life together be just as great?

"Guess I, ah, better get this upstairs," he said. "I was thinking it'd look good on that empty wall by the big picture window. That sound okay to you?"

"Perfect," she said. "Just perfect."

"CAL, HONEY," Allie said, adding socks and SpongeBob boxers to his suitcase crammed with Legos and Lincoln Logs and Matchbox cars. "Do you think you might need a few more clothes?"

"What for?" he said, tossing in two airplanes that'd

been recent gifts from his father. "I've already got some on."

"Yes, but…" She took a deep breath. Counted to five—who had time for counting all the way to ten? "We're going to be at your Aunt Gillian and Uncle Joe's for a long time. Four and a half days. Plus, you'll need pajamas."

"I'll just sleep commando. That's what Dad does."

Keeping a straight face suddenly became a monumental task. "Excuse me?"

"Billy says all marshals sleep nekked 'cause that's what *real* men do. Pajamas are for wusses."

"First off," Allie said, taking Cal's red flannel airplane pj's from his top dresser drawer, "just because you wear pajamas, does not mean you're a *wuss*. Second, it's none of your or Billy's business what your father sleeps in. Third, I don't think I want you associating with Billy."

"What's *ass-so-ciating?*"

"A fancy word for playing with," she said, tweaking his nose.

"Ouch," he said. "Don't do that. I'm too old."

"*Ex-cuu-u-use* me," she said. "From now on, I'll only touch you by invitation."

"What's that mean?"

"That you have to ask me to hug you."

"Oh. Yeah," he said. "That'd be good. 'Cept for nighttime hugs and kisses. You can just do that—as long as no one's watching."

"Thanks," she said. "I feel honored. Want these?" she asked, holding up his art set.

He shrugged.

"What?" she asked. "You don't like to draw anymore, either?"

"Billy says it's not very manly."

Allie growled. "I've about had it with that kid."

"Which kid?" Caleb asked, strolling into the room.

"Dad!" Cal bounced up and slung his arms around his father. "Do you know where we're going for Thanksgiving?"

"I sure do. You packed?"

"Yeah," Cal said. "But Mom's being mean and making me take dumb stuff like underwear and clothes."

"Since when are clothes dumb?" Caleb asked, grinning in Allie's direction. "I love seeing what kinds of stuff your mom's wearing."

"Eeuuw," Cal said. "That's gross."

Caleb shrugged. "Maybe so, but if your mom says you need to pack clothes, then you'd better get with it. Come on," he said, approaching the bed holding the loaded case. "How about taking half of these toys out, then you'll have more room."

"Okay."

Allie crossed her arms before heading out into the hall.

"What?" Caleb asked trailing after her. "Don't be mad at me. I packed all my undies and pj's."

She rolled her eyes. "You sleep in boxers." Just boxers. And miles of bare chest. She gulped. "For the record, this isn't about what anyone sleeps in," she said. "But the way ever since you showed up, Cal's changing. He never used to second-guess me. And he sure never hung out with kids like Billy."

"You ever stop to think that now that he has a dad, he also has the self-confidence to try new things? Meet new kids?"

Allie didn't have anything to say in response. In fact, to be fair to Caleb, she hadn't even considered the fact that what she saw as sass and a general lack of cooperation was really more a case of Cal flexing his wings. Probably a good thing. But was now the best time for him to learn to fly?

Caleb pulled her into a hug. "He's a great kid. He's going to grow up to be some biogenetic-something, make a million trillion bucks and buy us both early retirements. From where I'm standing, we've got no troubles."

"Ha," Allie said against Caleb's wonderful smelling, even better feeling, chest. "Easy for you to say. You weren't the one who was just forbidden from touching him—especially his nose."

"You mean that tweaking thing you do?"

"What's wrong with it? He's cute. And so is his tweaked nose."

"Babe…" Caleb kissed the crown of her head before groaning. "Us manly men genuinely don't like having our noses messed with. Nothing personal against you messing with it—just one of those things."

"Oh."

"You're not getting all sad on me, are you?" He nudged her back to take a look at her face. "Seriously, Cal hates it when you do that to him. It embarrasses him. Especially when you do it in front of Reider and Sam. A few weeks back, he asked me to talk to you about it, but I said the truly manly thing to do would be talk to you himself. Explain how he feels. Sounds like he wasn't real eloquent about it, but at least it's a start toward independence and free thinking, don't you think?"

"Yes," Allie said, "But I'm not going to admit it."

"Okay, then, how about I admit something to you."

"What?"

"You know how much you hate my job?"

Her heart thundered with hope. "You quit?"

Caleb rode out the wall of tension standing between them. "No."

"I'm sorry," Allie said. "Reflexive action. I've prayed for so long that—"

"It's okay," he said.

"No, it's not. I am sorry, Caleb. I'm trying to be okay with what you do."

He shook his head. "I'm so sick of that. You *trying*, Al. How long is my job going to be an issue between us? And a pretty lame one at that, considering how little action I actually see."

"How can you say that?" she hissed. "Have you conveniently forgotten how much danger you were recently in? Just standing around watching me?"

"Standing around watching you…" He laughed. "And who has the dangerous job?"

"You're just twisting my words. Trying to be obtuse."

"No, Allie, when I arranged to have the long weekend off, meaning someone else is in charge of watching over you and Cal, I thought I was being considerate. Thanks for letting me know that wasn't the case."

"MAN! THIS IS AWESOME!" Cal said, skipping from seat to seat in back of the endless limo Gillian and Joe rented for the occasion. They'd also been kind enough to send one for Allie's mom.

In front, a marshal drove. The black stretch model was flanked both front and back by still more marshals.

Fortunately for Allie, she only had one marshal to contend with. Although getting Caleb out of his funk and into holiday cheer was going to take some doing.

"Bud," Caleb said to their son, "how about picking one seat and putting on a safety belt?"

"Aw, man," Cal complained. "Why do I hafta wear a seat belt? Limos can't crash."

"I assure you, they can," Allie said, reaching over to buckle in Caleb as well, noting his dour look when her loose long hair brushed his cheek. She sort of accidentally brushed other parts of him with other parts of herself as well, then flashed him her brightest smile. "Buckle up for safety."

"That's not going to work," he ground under his breath while Cal fiddled with the limo's four flat-screen TVs.

"Geez! I can watch *SpongeBob* and *Scooby Doo* and *Fairly Oddparents* and *Rugrats* all at the same time! Aunt Gillian and Uncle Joe rock!"

"All I did was help fasten your seat belt," Allie said to Caleb.

He stared straight ahead.

"I'm sorry," she whispered in his ear. "Yes, I'd like nothing better than for you to quit your job and settle into a nice, dull—safe—private practice. We could do lunch. But since I know that's not going to happen, I'd like to at least thank you from the bottom of my heart for taking off Thanksgiving, and ask your forgiveness for my stupid, insensitive outburst back at the house. Okay?"

His only answer was a grunt.

"Look, Dad! We can watch wrestling and football and basketball and fishing! And there's big headphones for each TV!"

"Cool," Caleb said.

"And Mom, they've even got all your cooking shows! And look at all the fancy bottles they've got down here." With his sneaker toe, Cal could just reach the liquor cabinet door. "Can I have some of that?" he said, pointing to an amber liquid.

"No," Allie and Caleb said at the same time.

"Check the fridge," Allie said. "There's probably pop."

"Wow!" Cal said as if hitting the mother lode in the tiny square refrigerator just within his reach. "There's not just pop, but candy bars and peanuts and stuff! And I can eat all of this I want?"

"No," Allie said.

"Yep," Caleb said.

Cal just sat staring at them both. "Well?" he asked, looking hopefully toward his mom. "Can I?"

Allie took a deep breath, rested her head against Caleb's all-too-capable shoulder, then said, "That depends."

"On what?" Cal asked.

Allie said, "I get to watch one of my cooking shows on one of the TVs—and a decorating show on another."

"Yeah," Cal's father said, wrapping his arm around

her, fitting her more snuggly against him. "And I get to watch a western."

"Then that only leaves me one show," Cal said, his pouty lower lip practically on the limo's psychedelic-disco carpeted floor.

"Just think," Allie said with a grin. "You'll have that much more time to eat. Which reminds me, please pass me a Snickers and a Coke. Caleb? Want anything?"

He ducked down to steal a kiss. "I'll just have some of what you're having."

Cal shot them both a look of pure eight-year-old disgust. *"Eeeeeuuuuuw!"*

Chapter Thirteen

"How was the trip?" Gillian asked, taking Allie's coat, then moving on to the rest of the Logue men—including a big, lovable golden-haired dog named Barney. The marshals on duty had surrounded the exterior of the house—located in a ritzy Portland suburb—but Adam had come in, along with Caleb and Cal. After a round of hugs, Joe held the baby and Meghan cabbaged on to Cal, yanking him in the direction of her playroom. Vince and Beau were also in the elaborate marble-floored entry, making Allie and Cal's welcome more like a parade.

"Heaven," Allie said about their ride. "There were a couple times I think I was too comfortable."

"No such thing," Gillian said, taking her hand. "Come on. Let's leave all these guys to talk shop. You're coming with me to our spa day. There's someone in the midst of a pedicure who I think you'll want to see."

"Mom?" Allie raised her eyebrows. "Getting a pedicure?"

"I thought all of us girls could use a little pampering so I hired experts. Masseuses, manicurists, hair stylists.

I've got a friend who works at Saks coming over later to outfit us for Thanksgiving dinner."

"You're kidding, right?"

Gillian laughed. "I told you, Joe's company is *really* taking off. He's already given over ten million to charity this year. He says me and the girls are his other favorite charity."

"Sounds like you hit the groom jackpot," Allie said while they headed down a long, sun-flooded hall floored with intricately patterned mosaics. Tropical plants lined the walls along with carved wood benches.

Barney trotted along behind them.

Caw! Caw!

Something big and reddish swooped past, narrowly missing Allie's left ear.

The dog barked.

"What was that?" she said after her initial shriek.

"Joe's new passion. He loves birds. That one's Bongo. In the solarium, where we're headed, are a good half-dozen more. The nice thing is that all of these floorings and furnishings can be hosed down, so the birds don't need to be caged. They're not as tame as they otherwise might be, but they seem fairly happy."

Gillian stepped into a massive, glass-domed room that literally took Allie's breath away. "This is… I'm speechless." The ceiling had to be at least twenty feet high. The room was like stepping into a private island paradise complete with towering palms, a waterfall, exotic, heavenly smelling flowers in a rainbow of hues and a meandering stream culminating in a tranquil pool. Ethereal classical strings played from hidden speakers and seated alongside the pool swathed in a sumptuous pink towel and robe was Victoria Hayworth, Allie's mom. Sliced cucumbers covered her eyes while a model-handsome guy massaged her feet.

"Happy Thanksgiving!" Allie called out, almost afraid to speak again for fear of shattering the dream.

"Allie, hon! You're here." Victoria whipped the veggies off her eyes. "How was your trip?"

"Nothing special." Grinning, Allie shrugged. "You know, just my usual boring old limo."

"Here," Gillian said to Allie, holding out a tall, red drink complete with a hibiscus and orange garnish. "Drink up, then strip. There's robe for you in the changing cabana. It's high time we get you good and relaxed."

"Believe me," Allie said, sipping the sweet, fruity drink, "I'm already there."

Ten minutes later, Allie had traded her usual stodgy suit for a fluffy pink robe, and while her and her mother's fingernails were being painted by two drop-dead gorgeous guys, their feet were being alternately soaked in warm scented water and massaged with warm oil by another hunk.

Barney had fallen asleep beside the waterfall. The tennis ball he'd dug out from beneath a blooming yellow hibiscus rested between his paws.

"Relax," Allie's mom said, reaching out to pat her daughter's forearm. "You look tense."

From her hairstyling station, where yet another hunk snipped here and there on Gillian's honey-gold curls, she said, "I have to agree, Allie. Time for you to start guzzling that drink as it looks like rum is the only thing that'll get you out of court mode and into the mood for fun."

Relief shimmered though Allie. After all her worrying about things her mother might say, that was it? Relax? She glanced her mom's way.

I love you, she mouthed.

Love you, too, Allie mouthed back.

"I wish your father could see all of this," her mom said in a wistful voice, gazing up at an orange and red bird high up in the trees.

"Me, too," said Allie.

"I'm proud of you, you know."

"For what?" Allie asked, sipping her drink.

"Letting go of your fear, for at least trying. What happened to your father was a horrible accident. But if you continue to lock yourself behind a wall of doubts, you may never see the beauty around you."

Allie reddened. What her mom said was true. But did she have to say it in front of Gillian?

Caleb's sister cleared her throat. "Not that it's any of my business, but sounds like sage advice we should toast." Gillian raised her glass. "To beauty."

"To beauty," Allie said, thinking the woman who could quite possibly soon be her sister-in-law was beautiful, both inside and out.

After all three women had toasted with two more of the drinks that went down more like Kool-Aid than liquor, Victoria wandered off for a nap. As soon as she'd left the room Gillian asked Allie, "So are you and my brother planning a Christmas wedding?"

Mellowed by rum and the waterfall's gentle shush,

Allie said, "I wish. Guess we still have a few kinks to work out."

"Like what?" Gillian asked. "Maybe I can help?"

Allie shook her big, towel-wrapped head. "Thanks, but in our case, time is pretty much the only thing that'll make a difference." She gazed off across the room at a huge blue bird perched at the top of a red-blossomed tree more suited to the Amazon than Oregon. "I'm assuming your brother thinks I'm going to just up and disappear again—which is ridiculous. I've apologized repeatedly. Assured him leaving is the furthest thing from my mind. But no matter what I say, I keep getting the feeling that he doesn't quite trust me not to break his heart."

"Well, you did do that," Gillian said. "Oh, not that, being manly man and all, he's ever come right out and said it, but after you left, he was never the same. Now, though, I see part of that old Caleb returning."

Allie hung her head in shame. Would the pain of one bad decision ever stop hurting?

"Oh, sweetie," Gillian said, hopping up from her chair to enfold Allie in a hug. "The last thing I wanted to do was bring you down. What I meant to say was that thanks to you, I not only have an awesome nephew, but my brother back. And for that I'm grateful."

"But you're also understandably still bitter about having lost the last nine years," Allie bravely said.

"You know…" While her hairstylist stood patiently reading a magazine, Gillian pulled one of the cushioned pool chairs to the manicure/pedicure station. "At first, yeah, I was furious for what you'd done, but then

I looked at it from your point of view. It's not been all that long ago that I went through my own less than idyllic romance. Joe and I survived some treacherous times. And believe me, there were more than a few days I couldn't decide whether I wanted to kiss the man or strangle him. Sure, now, every day I pinch myself to believe I'm not living in the pages of a fairy tale, but it wasn't always that way." She sipped at her drink. "Allie, I know firsthand my brother can be a major horse's behind. I can just imagine you initially telling him you were pregnant. You were probably hoping for a reaction somewhere in the range of shock, soon overcome by wild elation and tears and a romantic proposal, am I right?"

Tearing up herself that finally, *finally,* someone had stopped to look at her side of the coin, Allie nodded.

"Okay, and so then my moose of a brother probably just stood there, dumbfounded. Hands shoved in his pockets, saying nothing."

"No," Allie said. "He did keep saying one thing over and over. That he'd make it right." She laughed. "Well, our baby wasn't an *it.* From the first day I learned I was carrying Caleb's child, I wanted him or her more than anything I'd ever wanted in the world. More than my law degree. More than world peace. I selfishly wanted this child to be the glue bonding Caleb and I together forever. But one look at his face after I'd told him the news, and it didn't take rocket science or even my law degree to tell me he not only didn't want this baby, he didn't want me. He didn't want us, and this stupid, storybook image I'd spun of the two of us living happily—"

"That's not true," Caleb said, stepping out from behind a palm. "I wanted the happy ending. I just wasn't as quick to realize it. I needed more time. But you were too damned selfish to give me even a week."

Gillian blurted, "Oh, for heaven's sake! She wasn't selfish, Caleb, she was hurt. She was afraid for you, and even worse, probably thought you didn't want her or the baby. What woman in her right mind would stick around trying to force a man to love her? It can't be done. It's like shoving a square peg in a round hole. And you saying you were going to *make it right?* What the hell was that supposed to mean?"

"Zip it, Gil." Caleb didn't give two figs that his sister thought he'd bungled the situation all those years ago. All he cared about was that the woman he loved—and yes, he did love Allie, most likely never stopped loving her—was sitting alone and fragile with a calendar hunk staring at her like she was the meat he was going to wolf down for dinner.

Swooping his bride-to-be out of the stupid toe-decorating chair and into his arms, Caleb said, "Sis, carry on this party without Allie. She'll be busy for the rest of the day."

Not caring that the remaining woman in the room and three men were gaping, Caleb took his curvaceous treasure outlaw-style in search of the nearest bedroom.

Barney, tail wagging, trailed after them.

"I LOVE YOU," Allie said, her words landing against Caleb's warm neck and cheek, reverberating back to her laced with his heady, all-male smell. "I'm not even sure how or when it happened—maybe my love for you never stopped. Maybe just now, when you busted in on all that girly stuff and just took me."

"I haven't *taken* you just yet," he said, heading for the winding staircase at the end of the hall. "First we have to find a suitable place… A feat which I'm beginning to think may be tougher than our patching things up."

She laughed. Hugged him that much harder, now certain she'd never again let him go.

"I thought you'd been here before?" she asked.

"I have," he said. "But they keep building new additions. If Joe and Gillian weren't always doing nice things for people, all their money would be disgusting."

By the top of the stairs, Caleb was breathing heavy.

"You can put me down, you know?"

"Nope." He'd leaned against a marble pillar. "Just need a second to catch my breath. And what're you looking at?" he asked the dog.

Barney cocked his head and wagged his tail.

"He thinks you're a goon for keeping up this macho act. Seriously," she said, squirming for Caleb to put her down. "I was impressed by the whole scooping me up and carrying me off into the sunset routine. But now that it's just us, you can drop me. You know—" she winked "—save your energy for *other* activities."

"Oh, don't you worry," he said with a big, naughty grin. "That portion of my anatomy runs on an entirely different battery pack."

"Well in that case…."

"Hey—" a voice sounding suspiciously like Gillian's said through the house's intercom system. "If there's a moose upstairs, barreling his way through my delicate antiques looking for a place to snuggle with his sweetie, go to the end of the main hall. Make a right. Go to the end of that hall. Make another right. Go through the double doors, and you two will have the whole wing to yourselves. Oh, and in case you're wondering who this voice belongs to—it's God. You two better get it right this time or else I might have to come down there and—" Gillian giggled. "Joe, quit. I was right in the middle of— Well, why didn't you tell me I was still pressing the transmit button. You know I've never known how to work this—"

The dog raised his ears and whined.

Allie asked, "Seeing how even Barney's apparently confused, did you understand a fraction of those directions?"

Caleb released a ragged breath. "All I really understand is that this house is too big to pull off a proper Wild West kidnapping. Would you really not be too upset if I put you down? I'm dyin'."

Beaming just being with him, she shook her head.

He set her to her feet, and she took his hand. "Come on you big weakling. I think our room is this way."

"THIS IS REALLY IT?" Caleb asked.

"These were the only double doors I've seen since at least a mile back." Save for a small sliver of light sneaking past drapes, the room was so dark that until they found a light switch there was really no way to tell if they were in a bedroom or gymnasium.

With both of them fumbling for a switch, it wasn't

exactly a stellar launch to their official bedroom reunion. But as high as Allie currently felt knowing that
finally both had forgiven and were ready to move on
with their lives, she didn't need champagne and roses—
just Caleb.

Lots and lots of Caleb.

"Ah," he said, "I think I might've found something."
He flicked one light switch, then two, then burst out
laughing. "You've got to be kidding…."

Allie took one look at their room and started laughing right along with him. "Looks like someone knows
you a little too well."

"Remind me to thank Gillian and Joe for this. Sorry,
Barn, but this is one party you're not invited to." He shut
the doors on the dog.

"Caleb? How come Barney can't come in?"

He kissed her hard and claiming. "Because tonight
you're mine. And I'm not sharing."

Dazed and totally, completely, head-over-heels in love,
Caleb's ridiculous answer sounded logical enough to her!

In keeping with Gillian's apparent love of fantasy-
themed rooms, their room had been done up to resem-
ble a Wild West saloon with the red-velvet-draped bed
sitting up on a small stage. There was even a swing over
the bar and a rack of costumes in case they had trouble
getting into the mood.

Hand in hand, they climbed the short set of stairs to
the bed, then past, beyond a curtain that led to what a sign
proclaimed was "The Watering Trough." Perched in the
center of smooth-washed river pebbles placed like tiles
was a barrel-shaped bubbling hot tub. In a couple of

nearby stalls, two stuffed animatronic horses appeared to be chewing straw. They were so real looking, Allie had to stroke a brown nose. Almost as soft as the real thing!

On the far side of the room were a sink and open shower with dozens of spray jets angled to hit all major body parts, and some that might've been previously overlooked.

"This is nuts," Caleb said.

"I love it," Allie said, sweeping open the red velvet drapes behind the hot tub to reveal an awe-inspiring view of a snowcapped Mt. Hood. "We should just stay here forever. The place is so big, Gillian and Joe would never even know we were here."

Caleb drew the drapes.

"Hey, what'd you do that for? All that sunshine felt nice." She winked and suggestively spun the belt to her robe. "It'd feel even better if you took off this fluffy towel with sleeves."

"I might be off duty," he said, kneeling to slip his hand into the part in her robe, then gravitate up her thigh, "but that doesn't mean I've stopped worrying about you. Francis and most of his thugs might be behind bars, but that doesn't mean you're officially safe."

She rolled her eyes. "Shut up and just go back to that new territory exploration."

"Yes, ma'am." He tipped his imaginary hat.

"You can do better than that," she said, dragging him upright, then back out to the saloon portion of their suite. "How about a real cowboy hat? And chaps. Mmm, yeah, nice leather chaps and nothing else."

Once she'd parked him in front of the costume rack,

he frowned. "The hat, maybe. But chaps?" He shot her a look. "Sorry. Ain't going to happen. Now this on the other hand…" He held out a red bustier with black lace trim. "Oh yeah, Daddy likes. Go put it on."

Hands on her hips, she said, "And all I get to see on you is a lousy cowboy hat?"

"Tell you what," he said, leaving her breathless with a teasing kiss. "You get your assets poured into that getup, and I'll see what I can do."

ALLIE HAD NEVER FELT more feminine. Silly. But for sure, all-woman with her waist cinched in and her heaving *bosom* thrust up and out.

She took a deep breath, eyed herself one last time in the cheval mirror located in the dressing room/closet that was bigger than her whole bedroom at home, then headed out to the saloon room to meet her man.

"'Bout time," he said, shuffling a deck of cards at one of four poker tables. He sat with his booted and spurred feet up on the table. Faded jeans hugged the length of his long legs, and on his chest was nothing but the muscles and dark sprinkling of hair God gave him. On his head sat the hat she'd requested—on his face, a slow grin beckoning her straight onto his lap.

"Damn…" he said with an appreciative whistle. "Spin around."

Face no doubt as red as the cranberries they'd be having for Thanksgiving dinner, Allie abided by his request, making sure she added plenty of flirty moves with her matching red-and-black parasol.

"Y-you look…" Still smiling, he swallowed hard.

"What's the matter, cowboy? Cat got your tongue?"

"You are without a doubt, the most beautiful woman ever created."

"Thank you," she said, heart pounding to be the recipient of such high praise. "You're not so bad yourself. I like what you did with the hat. Though you might want to be careful with those spurs…."

ALLIE GRIPPED the iron headboard, Caleb's shoulders, his back. But anywhere she grabbed couldn't ground her from the elated feeling of flight that strummed through her with each thrust. He was just as amazing a lover as she remembered. Repeatedly bringing her to climax in a myriad of ingenious ways before he'd even been satisfied once.

He'd had tricks she was still recovering from. Then, just when she'd been on the verge of throwing a good old-fashioned hissy fit if he didn't once and for all satisfy the hunger that'd been growing since the last time she'd been in his arms, he'd plunged inside her, finally fulfilling her every aching need.

"God, I love you," he said, nipping at her breast, kissing her throat, then moving up, up to cover her mouth with his, stroking her with his tongue.

"I love you," she somehow managed.

Faster and faster he rode, and she clung to him, surrendering in full. Here, now, her every dream came true. No more heartache. From here to the end of what would hopefully be very long lives, there'd be nothing but joy.

He rode harder still, and she bit his shoulder, pressing her fingertips into his back, sliding her fingers farther down. Helping him uncover still deeper, more intimate spots until the pleasure spiraling through her was too great to further ponder their wondrous act when all she could do was oh-so-willingly surrender.

"I love you, I love you," she said between kisses.

"I love you," he said, sweeping aside long strands of her sweat dampened hair. "Never leave me again. No matter what idiotic, bullheaded thing I might say."

"I won't," she said. "No matter what. It's you and me and Cal together for the rest of our lives."

"Don't forget anyone else who might happen along," he said, easing over to pat her belly.

"You in a hurry for more?" she asked.

He nodded.

"Good," she said, giving him another kiss. "Ever since having Cal, I've dreamt of the day when I could have another baby. Only this time, with you there to help me raise it."

"Tell you what," he said. "How about we hit the watering trough for a nice, long soak, then you get back on that swing and we'll see what we can do about getting our boy a little brother or sister."

Allie couldn't help but giggle. "I don't know. Think it'll hold?"

He lightly smacked her behind. "Only one way to find out."

Chapter Fourteen

"Hey, Mom and Dad," Cal called out from his innertube as he floated down the solarium's stream along with his cousin. "Where have you been?"

Allie gave Caleb a nudge. Considering the fact that they'd been holed up in their suite for a whole afternoon, night and part of Thanksgiving morning, someone had a lot of explaining to do. She nominated him.

"Gee, thanks," he said under his breath.

Luckily, the stream had taken Cal around another bend, momentarily putting off the need to answer.

"Yeah," Adam said from one of the cushy pool chairs. "Where have you been?"

Beau looked up from an opulent poolside buffet of fruits and an assortment of yummy breakfast foods. "Come to think of it," he said, "it has been a while since you two were last sighted."

"Knock it off," Caleb said to his brothers, slipping his arm possessively around Allie's waist to lead her toward the buffet. "Let's just say we had catching up to do."

"Cool," Beau said, reaching for a pancake.

"No," Adam said. "If you'd had to put up with these two and their constant bickering for the past few weeks, you wouldn't think this sudden reunion was cool, but more of a glory-freakin'-be. So? Does this mean me and the crew will finally get some peace?"

"First off," Caleb began, pitching a grape at his brother.

It fell to the tile floor where Barney promptly ate it.

"I hope there will soon be no more need for a crew— and in light of recent events, I'm officially taking myself off it. And second, nothing else me and Allie do is any of your stinkin' business."

"Yeah," Beau said. "But you've gotta admit that Wild West room is pretty hot. At least give us a rundown on which equipment you used."

At that, Allie shrieked. "You two are merciless! Caleb, can't you get them under some sort of control?"

He laughed. "Been trying every day of my life. At this point, I'm thinking we might just have to find them women of their own to do the job for us."

SITTING AT Gillian and Joe's endless Thanksgiving table in the stone-walled, Medieval-themed dining hall, surrounded by so many she held dear, filled Allie with bone-deep contentment. How long had she wished for a big, boisterous family? For the secret about Cal's existence to not only be out, but for Caleb to embrace the knowledge of his having a son? How long had she wished for something stupid like a real turkey? And here all of it was together at this one long table gleaming with polished silver and sparkling crystal and the delicious aromas that came from not just turkey, but ham and mashed potatoes and sweet potatoes and all the trimmings anyone could ever ask for.

Better yet were the people. Caleb and Cal. Gillian and Joe and their two little ones. Beau and Adam and Vince. Her smiling mom. Even Joe's first wife's parents, who were busy doting on Meghan and the baby.

What a magical day. What a magical life.

If only her father could be here to share her many blessings. Allie cleared her throat. "If you don't mind," she said, "I'd like to add to Joe's prayer."

"What was wrong with mine?" Joe asked with a teasing wink.

"Nothing and you know it," she said. "I—I just…" She pressed her gold linen napkin to already tearing eyes. "I'm sorry. It's just that this is the first Thanksgiving in a long time that I've had so much to be so thankful for. Yes, I've been blessed with a fine son and a great job and home, but this year, I'm almost too happy. I have this sensation like if I sneeze or something, all of this—you—might just vanish."

"Not a chance!" Beau said. "You see the huge lunch Adam put away? The boy's going nowhere soon."

Everyone shared a laugh, lightening the gravity of Allie's words. Yet in all of their faces, she saw recognition for what she'd meant. They were especially thankful, too. She saw it in the way Gillian rested her head on Joe's shoulder. The way Vince cupped his hand around the top of Cal's head. The way Caleb gave both his brothers affectionate smiles.

"Anyway," she said, swallowing the happy knot in

her throat, "thank you." She raised her wineglass. "Not just to all of you, but to God and all the angels. Thank you all so very, very much."

"Hear, hear," Vince said, and raised his glass in sharing her toast. Everyone else joined in, Cal and Meghan clinking their crystal goblets filled with chocolate milk.

"Mom?" Cal finally asked. "Can we quit talkin' and eat? Me and Meggie wanna get back in the pool."

"Yeah," Caleb said, shooting her a private look of such pure love she almost fell into a swoon worthy of a saloon girl. "This boy's got some major dunking ahead of him."

"All right," she said. "Thanks everyone for indulging me. Let's eat."

Adam said, "I'll give you an Amen for that!"

Barney, having been sitting patiently beside Adam, barked for his own share of the meal.

"WHAT AN AMAZING WEEKEND," Allie said, collapsing onto her living room sofa, glad when Caleb sat beside her so she could rest her feet on his lap. He'd stored quite a chunk of vacation time over the years and had decided to use the weeks before the wedding not only to relax and move, but file for an official transfer to Allie's judicial district. She still wasn't thrilled about Caleb's career choice, but was trying to at least be okay with it.

"Hey!" he complained. "I was just about to plunk my feet on you."

"Sorry," she said with a sweet smile. "I enacted my plan first."

He shook his head, reaching his hand out to hers, lacing their fingers. "This the way it's always going to be around here once we get hitched? You using me as a foot rest?"

"Oh, I don't know," she said. "There are lots of other parts I'd like to rest on you, too."

"Mmm…" His lips parted in a slow grin. "I'm liking the sound of this." He stroked the core of her palm with his thumb, streaking heat through her.

Eyes closed, she sighed. "Thank you."

"For what?"

"For letting go of the past. For the great life we have ahead of us."

"What if I turn out to be a royal pain in your derriere? Leaving my dirty socks all over the place and never helping with dinner?"

"I can think of worse things…" *Like you never having been here at all.*

"What's up with this sudden sad face?" he asked. "You having second thoughts?"

She shook her head. "This time we're going to get things right."

"Yeah," he said with a solid nod. "That sounds good. Real good."

"So then we'll take Gillian and Joe up on their offer to do this thing at Christmas at their house?"

"This thing?" He pouted. "You referring to our wedding—the most important day of our lives—as *this thing?*"

"You know what I mean," she said, squeezing his hand. "I don't know, it just sounds weird referring to it as our wedding. I'm afraid if I say it too much, I'll jinx us."

"Darlin'," he said, dragging her across the sofa to snuggle alongside him, "once I tell Gillian and Joe our wedding is on, believe me, it'll be like a speeding train. Nothing's going to stop it. In that palace of a house of theirs, not even the weather can bring us down. Trust me, we're good to go."

"All right, then…" After taking a shaky breath, she said, "Guess I'd better see how much Adam and Bear enjoy wedding dress shopping."

"How come they get to go and not me?"

"Ever heard of a little rule stating it's bad luck for the groom to see the dress before the bride wears it walking down the aisle?"

"Yeah, but seeing how we've already established the fact that we're home free as far as bad luck is concerned—"

"No," she said. She did kiss him, though, to soften the blow. "Sorry, but on this point, I mean business. We shouldn't mess around with tradition."

"But Gillian," Allie said on the phone a few days later. "Isn't it tradition for the bride to pay for the music?"

"Sure," Gillian said, "but I understand the full orchestra is somewhat over the top, and since I know how much Caleb adores all things country, I thought it might be fun to get a really big name in for the reception. You know, someone he'll never expect. Garth Brooks or Shania Twain."

"Assuming they'd even perform at a wedding reception, do you have any idea how much either of those two would cost?"

"Yes, which is why Joe and I would be honored to cover their fee. It'll be our gift to you."

"You're already providing the space, catering, flying in a photographer. Gillian, I know your heart's in the right place, but you're making me feel like a moocher."

"Puh-lease." Gillian made a *pfft* sound. "You'll have become a moocher when you're over here begging me for stuff. When I'm begging you to let me give you stuff, that's a whole other story. So? Who should I book? Garth or Shania? Maybe both? Oh—and don't tell Caleb. I want it to be a surprise."

"HATE TO BE the bearer of bad news," Allie said to Caleb that night as she flipped the six pork chops she was preparing for dinner. One each for Caleb, Cal and herself. Three for Adam, who'd said he was starving and forgot to bring a *lunch*. "But your sister is out of her mind."

"I like Aunt Gillian," Cal said from the salad-making station where he helped his dad tear lettuce. "She's fun."

"I didn't say she wasn't," Allie said. "Just that some of her ideas are a little…"

"Insane?" Caleb finished her thought for her.

"I was going to say unconventional. But I suppose your word works just fine."

"What'd she do now?" he asked, washing two tomatoes. "Please tell me she nixed the whole Cirque du Soleil ceremony theme? My ass was aching just thinking about what bizarre contortions I'd have to get into just to kiss my bride."

"Funny," Allie said, bursting into a laugh. "And true, but watch your language."

"I hear worse than *ass* at school, Mom. You should hear the kinds of stuff Billy says out on the playground."

"Thanks," Allie said. "But I think I'll pass. And you watch your mouth, too."

"Yes, ma'am. Hey, Dad?" Cal asked.

"Yep?"

"Can we go see *Power Force* tonight? Billy said this is the last week 'cause his mom has to make room for all the new Christmas movies. His mom owns the movies. Wouldn't that be awesome? That'd be like better than bein' president or a millionaire."

"Things have been pretty calm around here," Caleb said. "Sounds okay to me. How 'bout you, Al?"

"I'd love to go to a movie, but *Power Force*?"

"Billy says it's *very* educational."

"Thanks," she said. "But after hearing the sampling of foul language he's already taught you, I don't put great stock in young Billy's teaching recommendations."

"Cool!" Cal said. "That mean we can go?"

"WHY DID I LET YOU TWO talk me into that?" Allie said, shaking her head on the drive home. "That last scene. Ugh." She shuddered.

"High five, man." Caleb held out his palm to the back seat. "Sounds like we did a great job disgusting your mom."

"Yeah!" Cal said, meeting Caleb's hand with a solid thwack. "When that alien sliced Laird in half with his turbo sword, I thought he was dead for sure, but then…."

Allie settled back in her seat with a contented sigh. Though she'd never admit it, the movie had actually been pretty good. Of course, it hadn't hurt that Laird was hot! Plus, it felt wonderful getting back to normal life. How long had it been since she'd left the house at night without jumping through protocol hoops? Sure, their security detail was both in front and behind her sedan, but at least she was once again back in her own car, Caleb capably at the wheel, safely guiding them through a steady rain.

Mmm... His hands looked so strong curved around the wheel. They'd looked good doing other tasks, too. Good thing for the dark night covering her naughty, blushing grin!

How rare was it when life gave you a do-over?

How rare, and how wonderful. Why, why had she ever been so naive as to for all practical purposes throw Caleb away?

Rain drummed the roof while the back-and-forth swish of the wiper blades lulled her into a sleepy contentment the likes of which she hadn't felt since nine years earlier. Back when the most stressful thing on her mind was acing her midterm or making that month's rent.

Caleb adjusted the rearview mirror, tightened his grip on the wheel.

"Dad?" Cal asked. "Can you please turn on the radio?"

"No can do, bud. Maybe in a little bit."

"Aw, man. How come?"

"Now's just not a good time, 'kay."

"But—"

"Cal!" Caleb barked with uncharacteristic roughness.

He was back to looking in the mirror, then increasing their speed.

"Everything, all right?" Allie asked. "It's pouring. Shouldn't you slow down?"

"Nope."

He sped up even more. Dodged his way around two slower cars, then ran a red light.

"Caleb," she said with a white-knuckle grip on her door handle. "You're scaring me."

"Sorry," Caleb said from between gritted teeth, taking the next curve a good forty miles an hour over the suggested speed limit. "We've got company. Not sure where Adam's detail is." He tried talking into his mic, but got nothing but static. Was his brother out of range? Or worse?

"Cool!" Cal unbuckled his seat belt and hooked his arms over the front seat. "We being chased?"

"Not cool," Caleb said. "And I want both of you to get as far down as possible."

"Can I keep off my seat belt?" Cal asked.

"No!" Caleb and Allie barked together.

The car behind them—a large truck sporting even larger tires—sped up, coming still closer, revving the loud engine.

In the side mirror, Allie saw a long-haired man stick his head out of the truck's window, then his torso. In his arms, he held a rifle. "Oh my God, Caleb. He's got a gun. H-he's aiming right at us."

Chapter Fifteen

A second after fire flashed from the gun, a sharp ping sounded near the passenger-side mirror. Another at the trunk.

"Dammit," Caleb said, pressing the car still faster.

Allie couldn't breathe.

She seriously couldn't breathe.

Before, all of Francis's threats had seemed somehow distant and removed. Not really aimed at her or Cal. He couldn't *really* want to hurt her family. But now, with startling clarity, she saw differently—yes, the man not only wanted to hurt her and her son, but kill them.

Kill them.

As in dead.

A sob caught in her throat as she unfastened her seat belt, then began a frenzied climb into the backseat.

"What the hell are you doing?" Caleb cried. "Sit your ass down and buckle your safety belt!"

Cal started to cry. Really wailing. "Mommy said not to cuss. That neither of us is supposed to cuss."

Caleb swerved around a semi, then a slow-moving minivan.

Another shot was fired, this time shattering the rear window.

"Hellfire, how could I have been so freakin' stupid?" Caleb mumbled under his breath. "I'm a sitting duck. Got no radio. Got a piece, but how am I supposed to use it while weaving through this freakin' traffic?"

"Please God, let us be okay…" Allie chanted. "Please God, let us be okay…."

Caleb shot a glance in the rearview at Allie, who was white-faced and terrified, crouched in her seat, facing Cal, gripping his hand.

"We're all going to be fine," Caleb said to them both. "Hear that? Every damned one of us is going to be just fine. I'm going to make things right."

"Shut up!" Allie screeched through a teary, snot-filled, crazed laugh. "You said that once before. That you'd *make things right,* but—"

The shooter struck again, hitting the passenger-side back window.

"Cal," Caleb said. "Staying as low as possible, I want you to climb into the front. Allie, you, too."

Thankfully, they both did as they were told.

"We're going to get through this," Caleb said, sorry as hell for his earlier brusque tone. But it wasn't every day he had his wife-to-be and kid in a bind like this. "Trust me. We're going to be great."

Eyeing the town's state police headquarters, Caleb veered through two lanes of on-coming traffic to shoot for the lot. Guns blazing, Francis's dumb kin followed.

Fortunately, state cops weren't so different from other law enforcement types, in that they didn't take kindly to having their *house* and cars shot up.

In under a minute, Caleb doubled back to the relative safety of the station to off-load precious cargo before resuming the chase—only this time, he'd be the one doing the shooting.

No one fired on his family and lived to tell about it.

No one.

"Y-you're just going to leave us here?" Allie cried, clutching Cal.

"Yes!" Caleb shouted. "You'll be safe! Get inside!" Already, someone in uniform hustled out to usher Allie and Cal into the station.

The second Caleb saw they were in good hands, he shouted "Love you!" out the car window, then took off in hot pursuit—not only to find the shooter, but Bear and his brother.

If they were hurt….

Teeth clenched, all Caleb could think was that they'd better not be hurt. Or anyone who'd ever even spoken to Francis was going down—*hard*.

WAITING FOR CALEB, Allie paced, gnawed her nails. Cried. Paced some more. Above all, she couldn't help but compare this night with another. The awful night her father had been gunned down in the line of duty.

Closing her eyes, Allie went back roughly twenty

years in time to the top of the stairs from where she'd watched the scene unfold.

With her father already an eternity late getting home from his shift, Allie's mom had sat ramrod straight, knitting at a furious pace.

Her mother knit a lot, the speed indicating her mood. When she was content, her pace was leisurely. When sad, she slowed and made mistakes. And when she was mad, she worked even slower and made more mistakes, peppered with occasional grunts and cursing. Only one other time had Allie seen her mother knit as she was tonight—fast, with her rows perfectly straight—and that had been when Grandpa Ralph had been in the hospital having heart surgery. She'd been worried sick about him, as Allie presumed her mom was tonight about her father.

Allie's heart had seemed to beat in time with the needles' faint, harried clicks.

And then, at one-seventeen according to the grandfather clock in the hall, the doorbell rang.

Allie had jumped, but her mother, almost as if she'd been expecting the ding-dong, calmly set her needles and half-finished pink and blue afghan intended for Gladys Ulmstead's new grandbaby on the sofa beside her, smoothed her hair, took a deep breath, then answered the door.

Allie wasn't sure if her mother had sensed her at the top of the stairs, or if she'd made a noise, giving herself away. Regardless, her mother, lips pressed tight, had given her a funny half-smile, then walked outside, closing the door behind her.

Cold January air floated to Allie's hideout.

Allie had wanted so badly to run down the stairs and fly out the door, but she'd been frozen—not by temperature, but fear. And so she'd waited, until one of her father's friends, Officer Manny, had helped her mother back inside. Her usually strong mother had walked all hunched over, as if someone had socked her in the stomach. Another policeman Allie hadn't recognized followed her mom and Manny inside.

His expression grim, this stranger glanced at her, then shook his head before vanishing into the living room.

Again, Allie wanted to move, to demand her mother—*anyone*—tell her what was going on. Why these men were at her house in the middle of the night. But inside, she knew. She'd seen enough cop shows to know nothing good happened this late.

And so she'd pushed herself to her feet, and somehow gotten down the hall to the bathroom where she'd thrown up—twice—then sat on the cold tile floor in front of the toilet, leaning against the porcelain tub hugging her knees.

Daddy. Please, Daddy, come home.

Maybe he was just sick, and these men had come to take her and her mother to the hospital? But if that were the case, wouldn't they be rushing to see him?

No, she knew.

He was dead and never coming home.

Back in the present, the back door slammed shut.

Heart pounding, Allie's mouth went dry. Was Caleb home, or were strangers coming to tell her....

Though when she saw her dear Caleb, her insides turned quivery with relief and tears stung her eyes, she somehow managed to keep from leaping from the sofa and throwing her arms around him.

"You're back," Allie said to Caleb, never looking up from the living room fire. Outside, cold rain still fell.

Inside, it was raining, too.

It might sound corny, but when a girl cried as much as she had over the past few hours, surely it counted as its own storm!

"Cal all right?" he asked.

Swallowing hard, she nodded. "I let him sleep in my bed. Had to lay down with him for him to even try to sleep. He was worried about you." *So was I.* "How are Adam and Bear and the rest of the crew?"

"All good. Had their tires shot out. Guess because of the rain, we didn't hear."

"Yeah. Well, anyway, I guess you did a good job of driving."

"Thanks," he said, shrugging off his leather jacket, stepping into the fire's glow. He held out his hands to warm them, but the flickering flames were more about atmosphere than heat. "First thing after the wedding," he said, "I'm going to make this sucker into a real, wood-burning fireplace. It rains too much around here not to have a good spot to come home and warm yourself."

Allie started to cry again. She didn't want to, but

couldn't help it, anymore than she could help what she now had to do.

Caleb went to her, fell to his knees to cradle her face in his hands. "What's wrong? You said Cal's all right, so does that mean something's off with you? You're not physically hurt, are you? Just a little shook up?"

A little shook up? They all could've died! Tonight made the horror she'd gone through over her dad look like a cake walk.

She nodded.

"Sweetie," he said. "Sure, we had a little excitement, but—"

"Caleb, we were almost killed! People were *shooting* at us!"

He calmly reached for the box of tissue on the sofa's side table, held one to her nose, then said, "Blow."

She did.

"Better?"

She nodded, then shook her head. "I—I love you, but we can't get married. It'd never work."

"What?" He eased her back, smoothing stray hairs from her forehead. "You're clearly upset about tonight, but—"

"What did you do after you dropped us off?"

"What do you mean?"

"It's three a.m.," she said. "The movie was over at nine-thirty. Where have you been?"

He looked down.

"This is why I left you nine years ago, Caleb. Because of future nights like this. Only for Cal and I, hopefully tonight is the last we'll ever see of a world this out of control. For you, though," she laughed, "for you, this is ordinary. You actually enjoy it."

He froze. "You think I actually *liked* having my wife and kid getting shot at?"

"Of course not. You know what I mean. And I'm not your wife, Caleb. After tonight, I know I'm never meant to be your wife. My heart couldn't take it. As much as I love you," she said, crying all over again, "your job is just too dangerous."

"Oh, sweetie…" He pulled her back into his arms, smoothing her hair. Kissing her forehead, cheeks, nose and finally her lips. Just as seconds earlier she'd been drowning in tears, she was now drowning in love. In a kiss so savage sweet she couldn't breathe or think— just feel.

Heart pounding, she couldn't even imagine life without Caleb in it. But she also couldn't fathom a life strung with an endless succession of gun fights and wild chases. Never knowing if it'd be Caleb who came home, or some random marshal or police officers standing on the front porch, hats in hand, telling her, like they'd no doubt told her mother, they were sorry.

"It ever occur to you," Caleb said when they came up for air, "that at the moment, your job is the dangerous one? I mean, if it hadn't been for you and Cal's lives being threatened, I'd have never even come to Calumet City." Tenderly brushing her tears with the pads of his thumbs, he drew her to her feet, hugging her until she couldn't tell where she left off and he began.

Making a family with Caleb was all she'd ever wanted. But what was the point of making that family if all they ever had was tonight?

What would she tell Cal about why his daddy wasn't coming home? She knew from experience losing a dad was a hellish kind of pain. One she never wanted to see her son go through.

"I—I love you," she said, "but I can't marry you. It…" She looked down, toyed with a button on his denim shirt. It was the one she'd sewn for him. "It would just be too hard. I'm not strong enough."

Allie knew the moment she'd well and truly lost the only man she'd ever love.

Beneath her fingertips, his once warm, welcoming muscles turned to cold, unyielding stone.

He sighed. Clenched his jaw before looking at the pathetic fire, then back to her. "I've worked my ass off for you. I've brought you gifts. Tried working around the house. Made love to you till I thought I'd die if I didn't let go. But I held on, Allie. I held on for *you*. Because I always—*always,* put your needs—Cal's—before my own. You seemed skittish about the whole marriage thing. So, okay, fine. I took it slow. You were worried my family wouldn't like you. So okay, fine. I called in the cavalry so that even they bent over backward trying to please you. But know what I've only just now come to realize?"

Holding in new tears, she shook her head.

"With the benefit of hindsight, I see there is no such thing as pleasing you. The two of us could've been beyond great. We had it all. Only just like last time, you're throwing it away."

"That's not true," she sobbed. "You're twisting my words. I—"

"Save it," he said. "I've got a long night ahead of me to make it to Portland by morning."

"You can't leave. Not tonight. It's raining. It might be—"

"Dangerous?" He laughed. "I'd rather deal with rain any day than the likes of you. Tell Cal I love him, and will see him soon. Oh, and make no mistake, whether you want me in his life or not, I'm there. For good."

"DAMN." Caleb's brother Beau whistled. He sat in front of Caleb's Portland office desk while they went over the last of the history Beau needed to be caught up to speed on concerning Allie and Cal's security status. He would now be the lead man on their team. "Sounds like your Allie's one messed up broad."

"Don't call her *messed up*," Caleb bristled. "And she's not a *broad*, but the mother of my child."

"Still have a thing for her, huh?"

More like a blow torch. "No. I wouldn't care if I never saw her again."

"Uh-huh." Beau shoved his piece into his shoulder holster, then pulled on a leather jacket. "So how much longer this gig expected to last?"

"The judge and Cal will need protecting at least

through the sentencing phase of the trial. After that, I'm hoping Francis and his gang will back off—not that there can be many of them left."

"Yeah, you thought that the last time they hit."

Sighing, palm permanently clamped to his throbbing forehead, Caleb said, "Do me a favor?"

"What's that?"

"Get lost."

Used to his older brother's caustic flair, usually brought on by Allie, Beau shot him a grin. "Will do, big bro. Catch you on the flipside."

Caleb closed his eyes and groaned.

"ALLIE," Gillian said on the phone three days later. "Believe me, it's not the money I'm upset about, but you. You're not thinking clearly."

"Yes," Allie said, staring out her office window at the gloom. If Beau came in and caught her with her shades up, there'd be hell to pay, but at the moment, she really couldn't imagine a chewing out making her feel much worse. Since Caleb had left, a low-level queasiness seemed to have taken hold. Apparently, she was destined to feel wretched for the rest of her life. "I've never thought clearer. In fact, the point where I should've been concerned about being off my rocker was when I told Caleb I'd marry him in the first place. Dumb. Spectacularly stupid."

Gillian sighed. "Because you're clearly not yourself, I'm going to pretend I didn't hear that."

"Pretend all you want," Allie said. "But Caleb and I are finished as a couple."

"Just like that?"

"Yep."

"What about Thanksgiving?" Gillian asked. "You two seemed so in love."

"An illusion brought on by too much rich food and your indescribably beautiful house."

"It is awfully pretty, isn't it? Did I mention Joe hired a contractor to put in a small bowling alley? Just a small one. Three or four lanes at the most. But back to you, Allie. I seriously think you ought to reconsider backing out of this wedding. Shania was all set to come—though I made her promise not to flash her gorgeous eyes at either of our men—although Adam and Beau are both still available. Not that any sane woman would want them, but that's a whole other issue—"

"Gillian," Allie firmly said. "I've got to go."

"No," Caleb's sister said, perfectly picking up on Allie's deeper meaning. That once again she had to escape an impossible situation—even if it was only accomplished by shutting off her heart. "Allie, you don't have to go anywhere, ever again. Honey, don't you get it? You're home."

Despite being seated in her big judge's chair behind her big judge's desk, despite her insanely tight grip on the phone, a tremor shook through Allie. Low and deep and terrifying. Yes, she thought, making a bumbling goodbye, because of past mistakes and an uncertain future she couldn't even begin to navigate, she was now and forever alone. But at least her son wasn't.

SATURDAY WAS far too beautiful for it be early December in Oregon—at least as far as the weather was concerned. As for inside Allie's head, it felt snowy and ten degrees.

During the past two weeks, not a peep had been heard out of Francis or any of his men, who were now locked up with him. In fact, so many of Francis's buddies had been jailed, that, pending their own trials, they'd had to be transferred to neighboring counties due to a shortage of cells.

Because there couldn't possibly be more of Francis's following still at large, Allie stood at the upstairs hall window with the curtains wide open, staring out at Caleb and Vince as they bundled Cal into Caleb's black SUV.

Vince stooped to tickle Cal, and for the first time since Caleb had left, he squealed with laughter.

It was good hearing him laugh.

For him, it would be a great day spent at the petting farm, finally picking out that rooster he'd been carrying on about.

Allie hugged herself, wondering for the umpteenth time just what she was trying to accomplish by staying away from Caleb?

Squeezing her eyes shut, she imagined the feel of him holding her. Being inside her. Telling her he loved her. She imagined him wrestling, laughing with their son. The questions of whether or not he'd be a good dad or husband were gone.

He'd already proven himself awesome at both.

Leaving the only real question the cruelest one. If she abandoned herself to loving him, what if, like her father, she lost him? What would she do? How would she ever go on, knowing she had to not only deal with her own grief, but Cal's?

She clutched her still queasy stomach.

The back door opened. "Allie?"

Just hearing Caleb's voice stopped her heart. "I'm upstairs," she said.

"Close the drapes and step away from the window."

With her back to him, brushing silent tears, she did as she'd been told.

"Dammit, Allie, how many times do I have to tell you these guys play for keeps? We can't protect you if you're just standing there like the perfect target."

"Okay, okay, I get it." Blindly descending the stairs, she nodded. "Please, quit yelling at me."

"I'm not even *kind of* yelling," he calmly said, catching her with cool, professional detachment when she stumbled on the last step.

Just that brief touch was all it took to bring her well of sorrow crushing back.

"Beau and Adam are heading up your team here at the house," he said. "Bear's leading Cal's team."

"Wh-why not you?" she asked. *He's always been safe with you.*

He sighed. "I'm here just as a dad, Al. Give me a few

more seconds and I'll be out of your hair—just as you requested."

"Caleb, please, you're twisting my words."

"Save it. Save your tear buckets, too. As far as I'm concerned, you don't even exist."

That stole not only what was left of her crazy hope that they might at least be friends, but also her breath.

Didn't even exist?

Could he truly be that cold?

"Only reason I'm even in here," he said, "is to give my son's mother his agenda. On it are planned lunch and petting farm times. Assume a slight margin of error for unexpected bathroom stops and the like." He set the stark white paper on the black granite counter.

She glanced at it. At the military times. The typed names, addresses and phone numbers of Zippy's Pizza Circus and Ye Olde Petting Farm. This sheet couldn't be a product of the warmhearted man she loved. The Caleb she knew could never be this detached and impersonal. "Th-thank you."

Catching her with his precious sage green stare, he nodded, then headed out the back door.

"What have I done?" she whispered, staggering into a table chair.

She'd told Caleb she wouldn't marry him in some childish attempt to protect herself, but the fact of the matter was that she'd already lost her heart. And seeing him now, like this, every weekend and holiday, having him so close, yet indescribably far away…

In ways, wouldn't the pain be even more keen than losing him to—oh God, she couldn't even think it.

Wouldn't think it.

Raising the blinds over the kitchen sink, she watched the men she loved pull out of the drive, setting off on a fun day without her, picking out a rooster and hen without her. Laughing and loving and living without her.

Cradling her forehead in her hands, she laughed through more tears. What exactly were Beau and the other members of her team trying to protect? Because without Caleb in her life, she was no longer a flesh and blood woman, but an empty shell.

Chapter Sixteen

"You all right?" Caleb's father asked, joining Allie beside the fire. Caleb and Cal were out back, setting up the coop. It'd started to rain, and Vince had come inside, asking her to make a pot of coffee.

Gripping her mug tighter, she nodded. "I'm, um, just fine. Why wouldn't I be?" Pretending she was on the bench, forced to maintain a professional demeanor, she flashed the sweet man a smile. For if she paused for one second to think of Vince as the man who could've been her second father—too late, her smile faded and hot tears stung her eyes.

"Come here," he said, hand on the small of her back, gently guiding her to one of the lounge chairs. "I want to tell you a story."

Unable to speak, she nodded, cradling her coffee, angling in her chair to face him.

"My wife, the boys' and Gillian's momma, was one helluva woman. Helen made pot roast and gravy the likes of which made you sit up and sing. And her pies…" His face shone with a bittersweet smile. "Don't get me started. And Lord, the woman loved her babies.

I never saw any woman as protective over her kin—at least until I met you." He sipped his coffee.

"Sounds like you still miss her," Allie softly said.

"That I do. She was my best friend. But…" He shrugged. "Sometimes life deals crappy blows. I had to go on. Had four kids to raise, and if I'd done a bad job, Helen would've come back from the grave to wallop me good."

They both laughed.

"After me," Vince said, "I'd hazard a guess Gillian took her momma dying the hardest." He shook his head. "I don't know, could be I'm wrong. Grief's not the sort of thing you can assign numbers to. Figures and case-loads—those I was always real good at, but the touchy-feely stuff?" He chuckled. "Not my cup of tea. Anyway," he said with a deep breath, "all I was trying to get at in a not very direct way is that Caleb told me you don't want to marry him because you're afraid your whole lives are going to turn into one, big shoot-out, but honey…."

Caleb told his father her concerns? "My fears were personal," Allie said. "He should've never—"

"Whoa," Vince said. "Hold it right there. Us Logues—we're a family. One that if you had a lick of sense in that pretty head of yours, you'd soon be a legal part of. Technically, you're already one of us, but we'd just as soon make it official. As a family, we share what ails us, and Allie, my son is ailing over you. He has been for a long, long time. Now, I'm not one for digging up old bones, but my Helen spent an awful lot of time praying over my safety every time I went off to work, and apparently too little time praying for herself. While she was all busy, worrying herself about me being shot, she went and had a heart attack. My point is, you just can't tell what life's liable to bring. It's not like a light bulb or TV set. Doesn't come with a guarantee. All you can do is take what bits of happiness the good Lord gives you, and try to contend best you can with the rest."

"Mom, Mom!" Muddy and wet and obviously happy, Cal burst through the back door. "You've gotta come outside and see my rooster! Herbert's cool. And we got him some friends, too!"

Vince was in the den watching football, leaving Allie alone with her men.

"Cal," Caleb said, shutting the door behind them. "It's pretty nasty out. How about you get in the tub and your mom meets Herbert in the morning?"

"Th-that's okay," Allie said, hungry for more time with Caleb—no matter how awkward or unpleasant due to weather or his not wanting to be with her. "I don't mind getting wet."

"I do," Caleb said, fixing her with his new brand of icy stare. "Cal, seriously, bud, get those shoes off and head on up to the tub. You're starting to smell like a rooster."

"Are you and Grandpa spending the night?" Cal asked. "Smells like Mom's making Great-Grandma Beatrice's spaghetti."

"Sorry," Caleb said. "But I've got to be at work in the morning, and it's a long drive back to Portland."

"I thought you were going to work here?" Cal asked. "So why can't you now?"

A muscle twitched in Caleb's jaw.

Allie felt dangerously close to retching—even more so than usual.

Why didn't Caleb work here? Because she didn't want him to. Because, as usual, she was messing things up.

"Long story," Caleb said with an even longer sigh. "Come here," he pulled their boy into a fierce hug. "You know how much I love you, right?"

Cal nodded against Caleb's belly. "I love you, too."

"Cool. Then that means we're still on for next weekend?"

"Yeah," Cal said. "But how come you can't come back sooner? I'll miss you till then. What if something happens at school and I have to talk to you?"

"Well," Caleb said. "You can always talk to your mom, or call me. You've got all my numbers, right?"

"Yeah, but…" Cal's voice was small. "Please don't go, Dad. Just stay for Great-Grandma Beatrice's spaghetti. It's your favorite."

The watery-eyed glance Caleb shot her was Allie's undoing. What was wrong with her? Why wasn't she also begging him to stay?

"Sorry, dude. As good as it sounds, I'm afraid time out for spaghetti just isn't on my agenda."

"Okay," Cal said, hanging his head.

"No being sad," Caleb said. "Now, take off your shoes and run and say bye to Grandpa, then hop in the tub."

When Cal had gone, Allie approached Caleb, started

to speak, but he held up his hands in the universal sign of "back off."

"There's not a thing you could do or say to fix this, Allie. Don't waste your breath trying."

"But all I was going to—"

Cal was back with Vince in tow. Beau and Adam had also appeared.

While Vince and Adam horsed around with Cal, Beau and Caleb talked too quietly for her to hear off in the shadowy corner near the door. Were they discussing her safety? Or as Caleb no doubt saw it, her treachery?

Before she could ask, Vince and Caleb made their goodbyes, Adam and Beau trailing after them.

Cal headed upstairs for his bath, and she was once again alone—a place she was becoming all too painfully familiar with.

MONDAY MORNING, while Cal was upstairs getting ready for school, Allie stood at the kitchen counter, fixing oatmeal. Seeing how since she hadn't slept even half a wink, she was already dressed for work and made Caleb's favorite breakfast the old-fashioned way. Boiling it, then loading it with both brown sugar and white, butter, milk and raisins.

My mom made the best oatmeal. Loaded it with all the sinful good stuff. Lots of sugar and butter. Got me all good and warm before heading off to school. Mom was great about that kind of stuff. The colder the morning, the bigger her breakfasts.

Clutching the counter's edge, gasping on a sudden

racking sob, the full impact of what she'd done, what she was currently missing, hit her head-on.

Caleb was chuckling over some fond memory of his mom all the time. Just yesterday, Vince had reminisced about his wife. How much less full would both of their lives been without Helen's even brief time in it?

Allie knew then and there she was a fool.

But no more.

Jogging up the stairs, heart racing with excitement over her plan, she burst into Cal's bathroom at a dead run.

Out of breath, but smiling, she said, "Hurry, baby. I'm going to drop you off at school, then go get your dad. We have a wedding to plan and not a lot of time to do it."

"For real?" Cal asked, mouth foaming with toothpaste. "And then Dad's going to be here all the time?"

She nodded. "And let's get him a horse. Remember how he's always wanted a horse?"

"Mom?" Cal asked after rinsing his mouth. "You okay?"

"Oh, baby," she said, wrapping him in a big hug. "I'm better than okay. I'm fan-freakin'-tastic."

"Geez, Mom, you sound just like Billy."

"Yeah, well—" she ruffled his hair "—I feel a thousand times better. Come on, get dressed. Let's go. If we hurry, I should be able to get your dad back here in time to pick you up from school."

"Awesome!" He dried his mouth on a towel, then tossed it on the floor. And Allie was so happy, she didn't even care.

Bring on the mess.

Bring on the clutter.

Bring on the joy.

"But, Mom," Cal said from his room, T-shirt over his head. "What about Adam and Beau and the rest of the guys? Won't they be mad if we just sneak out?"

"Nah. Besides. I think any chance of danger is long gone by now, don't you?"

"Yeah. Let's go and be real sneaky. That way, Uncle Beau and Adam can be surprised, too."

AFTER MAKING a quick call to her neighbor and good friend Margaret, Cal and Allie stood waiting to get into Margaret's trusty forest-green Volvo.

"I'm happy to loan you the car," Margaret said, still in her robe and slippers. "But do you think leaving without your security detail is a good idea?"

Allie waved off her friend's concern. "I desperately want this day to be all about me and Caleb. Not his brothers and all their skulking friends. Besides, Cal and I will be fine. Francis and his thugs are safely behind bars. I don't even know why the government is still wasting money on having me and Cal protected."

"Maybe because you're worth protecting," Margaret said.

Allie gave her one last hug, made sure Cal had his seat belt on, then headed off for the best day of her life-at least until her wedding day!

"BE SURE AND BRING Dad back," Cal said in front of Byrd Elementary, half in and half out of the car. "I want him to see how much Herbert has grown."

"Okay," Allie said, giving him a hug and kiss.

"Mom, stop kissin' me!" he complained, making an awful face. "Want somebody to see?"

"Oh, of course not," Allie said with a laugh. "Wouldn't want that. Want anything special for dinner in case your dad and I get back in time to shop?"

"Ice cream? And get lots in case Uncle Adam eats it all."

"Yum. Sounds good to me."

"Hey, Cal! Catch!" A football slammed into the passenger-side backseat window.

Allie jumped, put her hand to her chest.

"Sorry, Mom," Cal said, scrambling after the ball. "That was Billy. He doesn't have a very good throwing arm."

"Oh," Allie said. Had Caleb taught him about throwing arms? In the past when she'd dropped him at school, he'd wandered off by himself, or with just Sam and Reider. Now, he was surrounded by a group of boys. If only she'd introduced him to his father sooner.

No, she thought, straightening in her seat.

No more looking back. No more regrets. What was done was done. For now and forever more, there'd be nothing but hope and happiness and love.

"Bye, Mom!" Cal said, slamming his door, then slinging his backpack over his shoulder to free up his hands to wave.

"Bye, bab—Cal!" She'd been on the verge of calling him *baby,* but looking at him now, running off to catch another of Billy's wobbly throws, she saw that he was growing into quite a handsome young man.

Hmm… Kind of like his father.

Just like the previous day when she couldn't stop crying?

Now, she couldn't stop grinning.

Carefully maneuvering out of the row of other cars filled with moms dropping off their kids, Allie relished the simple joy of being back in her old routine, then headed off to start her new routine—waking up every morning to a wonderful husband.

She made one last glance in the rearview mirror to check on her son, then screamed.

Slamming on the breaks, grinding the stick shift into Park, she tried yanking off her seat belt, but was stuck.

"Help! Someone please help!" she cried. "They're taking my son! Doesn't anyone see them? They're kidnapping my son!"

Two men dressed in jeans, dark sweatshirts and ski masks had hold of Cal and were hefting him into a dirty truck.

"Mom!" Cal yelled, breaking her heart. "Help!"

Finally she got free of the restraint, but it was too late, the red pickup, with its rear window blocked out by a confederate flag, was already roaring toward the end of the street.

A male passenger leaned out the window and started shooting. Once. Twice, he fired.

Margaret's windshield shattered.

Kids and grown-ups screamed.

Choked by exhaust fumes, Allie pulled herself together. She had to get to a phone. In her rush to escape her security detail, she'd also stupidly left her phone at home.

Halfway to the school stairs, she realized in a sort of

vague haze that her right shoulder stung. She cupped the pain, only to feel sticky warmth reminiscent of the type she'd felt that day in court. The day her face had been dripping in blood.

Not stopping to check herself, she ran on. Okay, apparently she'd been hurt. Maybe even shot. She'd worry about that later. Right now, she just had to get to a phone. She had to get help to save her son.

In a lifetime of idiotic mistakes, sneaking out of the house this morning—believing that just because Caleb and Adam and Beau and the rest of her team made her *feel* safe, that she actually was—had to be the dumbest, most careless, most—

The air was knocked from her lungs as someone tackled her just as she'd reached the school steps.

"Got her!"

"No-oo-o!" she screamed, kicking and fighting her captor. If they had her, how could she save her little boy?

"Allie! Stop fighting! It's me! Beau."

He had her around her waist and she sagged against him, sobbing uncontrollably. "Beau, please! Find Cal. You've got to find him. You've—"

"Shh…" he said, smoothing back her hair like his brother, sounding like his brother, even smelling a little like his brother. Only he wasn't Caleb. Could never be Caleb in a million years of trying.

Why hadn't she forced Caleb to stay last night? Why had she ever sent him away?

"Shh…" Beau said. "Everything's all right. Adam and Bear have Cal. Police have the goons who took him."

"Thank you," she said, trembling all over. "Thank you, thank you, thank you." When she'd calmed enough to stop crying, she said, "I have to see my son. I have to call Caleb. Tell him I'm sorry."

"Sure," Beau said, leading her to the school curb that was suddenly swarming with police and gawking parents and students. "All in due time."

"H-how did you find us?" she asked, allowing him to help her into the backseat of the now welcoming black SUV.

He laughed. "We were right behind you. Just let you think you were on your own. Hell, if something happened to you or Cal on my watch, my brother would have my balls." He winced. "Sorry to be crude, but it's the truth."

In the backseat, Beau beside her, signaling for the marshal driving to take off, Allie leaned against this man who would soon be her brother-in-law—assuming after her latest screw-up, Caleb would even want her as his wife.

"I love him so much, Beau—both of them. Your brother and Cal."

"I know," he said, awkwardly patting her leg.

"I just wanted to be on my own to tell him. You know, figured it would be more romantic, but…."

"It's okay," he said. "Dumb, but ultimately, no harm done."

Easy for Beau to say, but what if there had been harm done? Cal was now safe, but what about her future with his father?

"Beau?" Allie said right before her world started a slow fade to black.

"Yeah?"

"I forgot to tell you…. I think I m-might've been shot."

THAT NIGHT, exhausted after an endless day of police questioning and paperwork and alternating fury with Allie and love for her, Caleb helped her tuck their brave son into his bed.

Thank God, the shooter's bullet had only grazed Allie. The emergency room doctor surmised it was stress, not loss of blood, that caused her to pass out. The only first aid she'd needed was a squirt of antibacterial cream and a bandage. As for Caleb, after hearing the initial news that she'd been shot—he'd needed a gallon of antacid and a defibrillator!

"Sure you're all right?" he asked his already half-asleep kid.

"Yeah. Only my stomach kind of hurts after all that ice cream."

Caleb ruffled his hair. "I believe it. We all had to eat fast to get it away from Adam."

"Yeah," Cal said, yawning, then rolling onto his side and shutting his eyes.

Caleb's breath hitched, thinking what a close call they'd all had today. No matter what Allie said, he should've never left. No one could watch over the two people he most loved like him.

But then in Allie's case, the person she most needed protecting from was herself.

She kissed their son's cheek, and in the process got too close for Caleb's emotional comfort. The woman smelled the same—soapy and good. Felt the same—soft and warm. Only trouble was her insides had turned out to be about as cozy as a brick.

After Cal drifted off to sleep right before their eyes, Caleb got up, gesturing for Allie to precede him to the door. He left Cal's airplane lamp on, just in case he woke up spooked. He'd taken the kidnapping amazingly well. Maybe too well. The only thing that would tell them for sure was time.

"Thank you for getting here so fast," Allie said out in the hall. "It meant a lot that all of you could be here with him."

He shrugged. "Thank Joe. He's the one with enough cash to charter helicopters to fly the whole crew over." Gillian, Joe and the kids were now at the Morning Glory Inn for the night, after assuring Cal they'd be back first thing in the morning.

Together, silently, they trudged down the back stairs and into the kitchen.

"How long are you going to do this?" she asked.

He opened the fridge, staring blindly into the jumble of Chinese food take-out cartons. "Do what?"

"Give me the cold shoulder."

"Rest of our lives I guess. Not much else I can do."

"Do you even care why I tried sneaking past your brothers?"

"Nope." He reached for the leftover sweet and sour pork.

"Well, I'm going to tell you anyway. I wanted it to be just the two of us when I showed up at your office or apartment or wherever I had to find you in order to spill my heart out and basically grovel my way back into your life. I love you, Caleb. I love you no matter what you do. I get it that you love me, too—or at least you used to. And that because you love me, you're not going to go out of your way to do something stupid like get yourself hurt."

He slammed the food in the sink. "That's rich. For you to stand there telling me you trust me not to be stupid about getting hurt when you're the one who actually got herself shot. How could you be so careless with not only your life, but our son's? Do you realize that if my brothers hadn't been tailing you, odds are we might never have gotten Cal back? You might be dead? Why, Allie? Why the hell would you ever do such an asinine thing as sneaking out of here without protection?"

Crying, she stammered, "D-didn't you hear me? Because I love you. I—I wasn't thinking straight. I want to marry you. Spend every day of the rest of my life with you. It was like I had tunnel vision. All I could think of was getting to you. Begging you to give me a what? Third or fourth chance. B-but I guess I blew that, too."

Ashamed for letting her go on crying this long, Caleb drew her into his arms. "God help me, I'd give you a thousand chances, woman. Sometimes I have to wonder why, but I love you. I *seriously* love you."

Kissing him, laughing, crying, she said, "I love you, too."

"Okay, but listen." He cupped her cheeks with his big, protecting hands. "In order to avoid any future misunderstandings, we're getting married. Now."

She nodded. "Yes. Now. We won't even wait for Christmas."

"Agreed." He kissed her hard and claiming and soft and every way in between.

"But what about Gillian? She was planning a big Christmas wedding."

During another kiss, Caleb emitted a low sound somewhere between a groan and growl.

"Okay," Allie said, getting the hint, *loving* the hint. "Let me go call one of the county's other judges."

UPSTAIRS, peeking through the slats in the stair rails, Cal grinned. Whew. Finally his mom and dad were back together.

Good thing, too, 'cause he was really getting sick of always having to ask Clara for advice. People were starting to think she was his girlfriend and that was just wrong! Girls were okay to have as a mom and aunt and cousins and stuff, but as girlfriends? Yuck!

Epilogue

Joe put his arm around Gillian and squeezed. "Would you quit pouting. This is a beautiful ceremony. Look how happy they are."

"I don't care," Gillian said. "I had big plans for their wedding. Now I'm going to have to wait forever to have a big, fancy Christmas wedding at our house. You know about my mom's holiday wedding list. If only my brother could've waited a few more days."

Joe sighed, kissing the top of her head. "There's always Meghan's wedding. Why not start planning now?"

"Ha ha," she said, jabbing his ribs, eyeing the bride and groom. "Vegas. It's not a fit place for a wedding nine years in the making."

"Then how about the two of us just have a second wedding? Would that make you happy?"

"Really?" She beamed.

"I was about to say, 'no, not really,' but damn, you have a gorgeous smile."

"Thank you," she said, kissing him just as the happy couple shared their official first kiss as man and wife.

At the business end of the ivory rose petal-strewn aisle, Allie sighed with happy pleasure.

No one had ever had such a beautiful wedding.

Gillian and Joe, and a fleet of private jets, had seen to it everyone she loved was there. Her mother, all of Caleb's family, her security crew, her neighbor Margaret and Margaret's husband, Mike. Even Allie's work friends.

Seeing how they hadn't been able to find a judge willing to marry them in the middle of the night, Joe— being Joe—had just phoned some friend of his in Vegas to help plan a sunrise ceremony.

It'd been idyllic.

Hundreds of candles and ivory-colored poinsettias and fragrant ivory roses and an ivory satin gown for her, and jeans, boots, a dinner jacket and a starched white shirt for Caleb. He also sported a cowboy hat at her request. Cal's outfit matched his dad's.

After sharing congratulatory hugs and kisses, Allie practically floated on Caleb's arm into her dream reception. Equally elaborate, complete with a fancy breakfast, dancing, mimosas and even Caleb and Cal's favorite oatmeal!

Giselle seemed to be having an especially good time, still working her feminine wiles trying to break through Bear's all-business demeanor.

At the end of their tenth slow dance, Allie sleepily rested her cheek on Caleb's chest.

"Tired?" he asked.

"Yes," she said. "But in a wonderful way."

"Yeah," he said. "I know what you mean. Hungry?

Thirsty? Those champagne thingees are pretty good. Want me to get you one?"

She shook her head. "Probably not a good idea."

"How come?" Caleb asked, gently swaying to the soft ballad's beat. He froze. "No way. Already?"

"I'm not a hundred percent sure," she said. "But I have been feeling a little *off*. Last time I felt this way was… You know."

"Wow." He buckled, grabbing his knees.

"Caleb?" she asked, voice shaky with concern. "You all right?"

"Sure." He straightened. Cleared his throat. "Give me a minute. Last time this happened, I handled it bad. I need time to think. You know, be sure I make things right."

Allie wagged her sparkling new ring. "Thanks, but you pretty much already did."

* * * * *

*Watch for Beau's story,
the next in the U.S. MARSHALS series,
coming April 2006 only from
Harlequin American Romance.*

American ROMANCE®

A THREE-BOOK SERIES BY
Kaitlyn Rice

Heartland Sisters

To the folks in Augusta, Kansas, the three sisters were the Blume girls—a little pitiable, a bit mysterious and different enough to be feared.

The three sisters may have received an odd upbringing, but there's nothing odd about the affection, esteem and support they have for one another, no matter what crises come their way.

THE RUNAWAY BRIDESMAID

When Isabel Blume catches the bridal bouquet at a friend's wedding, and realizes her long-standing boyfriend has no intention of marrying her, she heads off to spend the summer at a friend's Colorado wilderness camp. There she meets the man whose proposal she really wants to hear. So why does she refuse him?

Available February 2006

Also look for:
THE LATE BLOOMER'S BABY
Available October 2005

THE THIRD DAUGHTER'S WISH
Available June 2006

Available wherever Harlequin books are sold.

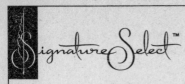

A breathtaking novel of
reunion and romance...

THE
F RTUNES
OF TEXAS:
Reunion

Once a Rebel

by Sheri WhiteFeather

Returning home to Red Rock after many
years, psychologist Susan Fortune is reunited
with Ethan Eldridge, a man she hasn't gotten
over in seventeen years. When tragedy and grief
overtake the family, Susan leans on Ethan to
overcome her feelings—and soon realizes that
her life can't be complete without him.

Coming in February

Silhouette®
Where love comes alive™

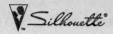

SPECIAL EDITION™

presents a new continuity

FAMILY BUSINESS:

Bound by fate, a shattered family renews their ties—and finds a legacy of love.

Don't miss a single exciting title
from *Family Business:*

PRODIGAL SON
by Susan Mallery, January 2006

THE BOSS AND MISS BAXTER
by Wendy Warren, February 2006

THE BABY DEAL
by Victoria Pade, March 2006

FALLING FOR THE BOSS
by Elizabeth Harbison, April 2006

HER BEST-KEPT SECRET
by Brenda Harlen, May 2006

MERGERS & MATRIMONY
by Allison Leigh, June 2006

Where love comes alive™